GIDEON

FALL FROM GRACE

S. HAMIL

S. Hamil's Book List

PARANORMALS

GOLDEN VAMPIRES OF TUSCANY SERIES
Honeymoon Bite Book 1
Mortal Bite Book 2
Christmas Bite Book 3
Midnight Bite Book 4

THE GUARDIANS
Heavenly Lover Book 1
Underworld Lover Book 2
Underworld Queen Book 3
Redemption Book 4

FALL FROM GRACE SERIES
Gideon: Heavenly Fall

All of S. Hamil's books are available on Audible,
narrated by the talented J.D. Hart.

ABOUT THE BOOK

He's a vampire-angel hybrid. She's the guardian angel who ruined his life. Is it a match made in Heaven…or Hell?

Start an unforgettable paranormal series from the dark, twisted New York Times bestselling author S. Hamil and her less twisted alter-ego, Sharon Hamilton!

GIDEON can no longer stand his post as a Watcher above the Golden Gate Bridge. When the half-angel, half-vampire rebels by transforming the San Francisco skyline forever, he's forced into a life on the run. Everybody seems to want a piece of him, from The Supreme Being to a vampire queen hell-bent on making him a sex slave…again.

As Gideon struggles for survival, he begins falling for the angel who ruined his bloodsucking days by saddling him with wings in the first place. But can a freak like Gideon ever find happiness when love is forbidden? Will his beloved inspire his salvation…or destroy his life all over again?

GIDEON: *Heavenly Fall* is the first book in the Fall From Grace saga, a series of dark paranormal romance novels. If you like fast-paced adventure, witty barbs, and sizzling romance, then you'll love S. Hamil's captivating tale.

THE LABYRINTH

"THERE IS A symbol that started with the angels. You won't find it in churches or cathedrals, but it is ours, nonetheless."

His warm brown eyes nudged their way into her heart, his dark lashes fluttering up and down as he spoke, fanning the flames of her desire for him to take her again.

"What is it?" she asked, afraid to speak, breaking the warm space between them.

"Guess."

"Give me hints."

He smiled. "An angel in quiet contemplation, bowing in reverence to something more precious than life itself."

She closed her eyes. "I can't see it. I see the angel, but I don't see the symbol."

"Watch." He delicately held the pink fingers of her right hand, and softly pressed them around a No. 2

yellow pencil that suddenly appeared. He leaned in to her, his chest against her back as she sat on his lap, his other arm gently residing on her left hip. The simple, intimate act was stirring. She inhaled deeply as he pressed the graphite vein to the smooth white vellum of the sketchbook materializing on the table. The scratch became an arched curve, like a backwards comma.

She'd seen that pattern before. It was the line of radiance the orange sunglow gave to the outline of one wing, as he stood in a golden field late in the afternoon.

A smile slowly curved the ends of her lips. He was watching every movement she made. Her mouth felt naked and quivered to mate with his. He lowered his head, his long sensual fingers still cradling hers on the page. Her breathing became notched and ragged as his face approached hers and she drank from the softness and the wonder of their love. His warm flesh melted in to hers and her mouth opened to him, like her soul opened to him to touch her in every way.

When he pulled back, she was filled with loss. He focused down to the drawing and applied pressure to her fingers again.

"And now for the other one," he whispered.

Under his slow, deliberate tutelage, he made another curve the opposite to the first one, beginning and ending by touching the two corresponding spots of the other image.

And there it was, the symbol she would forever associate with angels until her last days:

A heart.

It wasn't a symbol of death or sacrifice. No struggle. Part curved, part straight. Two halves becoming one, touching identical places on the other and becoming one whole symbol from two separate and distinct parts, something neither could do without the other.

She had seen him stand in front of her naked, with his head bowed and his wings looming above, arching with grace. His strong shoulders would cast a shadow of power over her, his head lowered in complete and utter devotion.

Pure love.

Gideon's love.

Everlasting love.

CHAPTER 1

T HE MONSTROUS PURPLE bus barreled down Highway 101 at eighty miles an hour. Multicolored block letters were shrink-wrapped onto the hulking frame: Blood Bank of the Redwoods. Gideon was still shocked it had been so easy to steal the beast. Flapped his wings and showed his fangs, and the technician was out of there.

Motivating the decision today to take his life into his own hands, he was completely done with being isolated, separated from all the other Guardians called to missions by "Father" in his infinite wisdom. *Father* was not nearly the right name to describe the heartless codger he labeled Supreme Being, or SB. The only mission given to Gideon was to watch and report. Be a spy on the civilian population.

A Watcher wasn't a doer.

Like all the other Watchers before him, his job was to help the Guardians save lives, and by saving lives they saved souls.

He'd seen thousands of them carting the civilians' precious cargo, their red elixir of life. Gideon had always wanted to drive one. Today had been a true Red Letter Day, the best day of his life so far. Coming over the Marin grade, the stainless-steel beast almost leapt off the pavement like a skateboard as the freeway suddenly made a steep dip, heading toward San Francisco.

Happy to be down off his perch atop the North Tower of the Golden Gate Bridge where he had spent the last fifty years of his immortal life, Gideon was finally looking forward to a future carved by his own hand. Probably a dark one. When earlier today he'd used his wings, searching for the bus in Marin, they were white, as all Guardians' wings were, but he suspected by sunset they'd turn black.

Worst, coldest fuckin' job in the universe. Did the Supreme Being hate him that much? And what had he ever done to deserve this? Could he help it if he saw the human population as flesh sacs? That's what they were. He was tired of pretending, holding back his true vampiric nature. He had to stuff down his urges so he wouldn't become a piece of scorched meat buried in Heaven's graveyard somewhere. None of it was easy, with the incessant singing and Guardianship classes in gardening and lacemaking, which nearly drove him insane. Maybe he was insane. A person *would have to be* insane to be *that* happy and cheerful all the time.

Fuck that shit.

He was bored to death. It took a saint to endure that kind of life. He'd even begun to bring heavy weapons to work with him like he was looking for a large enough target to use them on. He had fantasies about taking down a blimp or a cargo ship.

I'm an angel messenger all right. I'm going postal.

Being stuck there was worse than being ignored. He was buried. Buried alive in the human world on top of the coldest fuckin' bridge in the state, the only heat coming from the glow and meager warmth of the red lamp sitting beneath his butt on his perch atop the massive metal structure. The Supreme Being was cruel, and contrary to what the Guardians preached to him, SB did not know the meaning of the word compassion. Or pleasure. Or ecstasy.

Why leave him up there alone to suffer? He knew the asshole was watching, could feel His eyes on his back. Probably the kind of guy who liked to pick the wings off flies and watch them run around chained by gravity. Tasking Gideon an eternity to make calls to Guardians so they could swoop down in their gossamer-winged finery and save humans from jumping?

And be okay with letting them get all the credit for the "saves"? The celebrations of their victories were the worst. Cherub choirs hurt his ears with their incessant clapping and yodeling in preternatural form humans couldn't hear.

No, the Golden Gate Bridge might be a little better than Heaven. But just a little.

Harkening back to his old vampiric nature, he'd taken to counting again. It was what he did when he was nervous or when things weren't going his way. He'd count ships that passed underneath. Count the cruise ships to Alcatraz. Count the freighters, the rice rocket cargo ships, and the dirty tankers. He even counted the number of cargo containers and grouped them into types by color, size, and branding. Occasionally, he'd get to count a pleasure yacht or sailing ship. What was he supposed to do? Pray? What a useless waste of time.

Sometimes he'd go days without a jumper. Others, there could be a handful. They seemed to run in bunches, like grapes. Perhaps it was the pattern of the "circle of life" in the human world. Or the Pacific Ocean's currents or winds. Perhaps the pull of the moon or pollution or traffic. Who knew?

Let 'em jump. If they want to die, let them rest in peace. Float a target out there so they can hit the bull's eye—go out with a perfect score, so to speak.

And then there'd be one asshole who'd miss and spend his last remaining seconds feeling a complete failure. He hated sharing their angst, something he was fully privy to. The fear was one thing he could tolerate, but their regrets, who needed it? He had enough of his own, enough for the whole human race and half the vampire race as well.

No, going out, missing the imaginary target and scoring a fuckin' zero was the way to go. They were losers anyway. Might as well claim that last desperate act as a loser.

He was living proof not everyone wanted to be saved. He'd always thought vampires would wind up in the Underworld. But no, that wasn't the way of Heaven, and it wasn't his destiny. Just as not all the jumpers were saved, not every vampire wound up down below. What made him so special, he wondered. So what if a bunch of the human population and a few vamps wanted to end themselves?

No, Gideon thought, redemption was a dirty word and highly overrated.

He'd seen the Guardians' super sanctimonious smiles while they fluttered back up to Heaven in a shower of golden sparkles. He'd seen them arrive home to a cheering crowd of angelic hoards and cherub choirs that hurt Gideon's sensitive ears. And never once did any of them stop and bother to say thank you to him. Not once.

What's up with that?

Maybe they knew about his bloodlust. He knew SB understood, but he wasn't sure about the Guardians. It had been one colossal fuckup, turning him into an angel. He wasn't capable of dying anyway, and he probably wouldn't have even if some damned Guardian hadn't decided to show mercy on him. The little do-gooder thought his wounds were life-threatening, that he'd been trying to save the young lady when he was actually going to drain her after he'd pushed her out of the way of the truck that clipped him. Miss-Goody-Two-Shoes fucked up his whole life. He'd been swooped up, fitted with wings he never wanted—he already could fly—"saved" they called it. More like fucked. And not in the way he liked, either. This was the fucking kind of fucked where the fuckee didn't leave with a smile on his face.

His days in Heaven were tortured with music, which gave him migraines. The sunlight burned his eyes. How he'd like to drain the lifeblood from all their chubby cheeks.

He thought about the nubile young Guardians, especially the redheads, turned in their prime. Their lusciously smooth bodies definitely had heavenly curves. He lived in a state of stiff arousal those long years of his angel training classes, in such close proximity to such lovely, naïve creatures. His sensitive skin craved to touch them as his fangs yearned to plunge deep and coat his throat with their sweet lifeblood. His ears had buzzed and his nose itched 24/7.

Their scent was addicting. It would only be a matter of time before the warnings and spells would no longer work on him, and he'd do his share of rutting through the entire redhead population. And that would never do. But it might have earned him a ticket down below. He was counting on that today. He wanted out of a life he never chose, but hoped he could alter.

So he was going to leave in a blaze of glory. Catch the attention of the Guardians who had ignored him for so long. Steal a Blood Bank bus, suck out the entire inventory, and send it over the edge. Go commiserate with his buddies down below where he heard the action was much better and the climate more to his liking.

Supreme Fucktard must have known he'd have a breaking point. So maybe that's why they'd sent him up to the top of the North Tower. At first, he was relieved to be away from the choirs and angel dust, standing up above the fog line like he was in charge of the whole bay. But, as the years went by, it got worse and worse.

Even though they gave him an estate in Sonoma County where he could play around with winemaking on his one day off, he was utterly and completely bored. Making wine wasn't at all like what he remembered of making love. He should have used his estate as a love nest. Perhaps they would have overlooked his indiscretion, violating the directive never to bed a female of any sort as long as he remained angel.

Well bugger that.

Practically no one ever visited him except his angel friend, Francis, the ex-Priest who took his Sunday shift. All his other friends had screwed up and been spirited away to the Underworld years ago. Francis just had to make sure he didn't get too drunk and fall off that North Tower. That would surprise a commuter. A drunken Guardian on the windshield on the way to work? That was actually something he'd *like* to watch. Francis's old angry Russian friend had nearly done that once.

Gideon spent his other six days counting whatever passed by him or through the straights, even seagulls. He knew how many houseboats and boats were anchored in Sausalito on any given day. He'd count cars, then just red cars, cars with ski racks, cars with barking dogs, cars with women who hiked up their skirts so high he could see all those private parts eternally denied him.

So maybe SB had a plan. If he did, Gideon would be the last to know, that was for sure.

Does he even freakin' know how freakin' cold it was up there?

The purple beast veered when the freeway took a sharp turn to the left. The sloppy box-like manufacture of the vehicle was becoming more difficult to control the faster he went. Sticky dark red blood was leaking from the crack at the base of the enormous mobile Blood Bank's rear doors. Gideon had been tossing back empty bags of plasma after he'd torn off the tops and drained them. After fifty years, the blood still made him hard. Harder than one of those fucking towers, and just as tall too.

Definitely going to have to do something about that. He'd be in some real pain in an hour.

He finished a bag and tossed it through the blown-out driver's side window. He watched through the side mirror as the long red finger of blood swirled in the air behind him until it landed on someone's windshield.

To a motorist from behind, it would look like the doors themselves were leaking. The blood began as droplets, but soon cascaded in ribbons and flew in the breeze like little red snippets of flags as the bus swerved.

Hard to peer through blood-soaked wipers when you're going at sixty-plus miles per hour, he thought, as he saw drivers behind him deal with the visibility issue, probably thinking they'd hit a bird or some other animal. Scanning his side mirror again, he spotted a vehicle pileup several hundred yards behind him, amidst smoke and steam. It managed to block a California Highway Patrolman. His red light flashed impotently behind the mound of cars acting as a barrier, while Gideon's bus sped along to relative safety, if that's what it could be called.

To infinity and beyond.

Gideon smiled. This was turning out to be a nice day, after all. Causing havoc lightened his mood. Being invisible for so long actually made him giddy to create such a splash. And how the news media would play this one up. Yeah, it was going to be fun watching all that. He was going to get a motel room in the city, eat In-N-Out burgers and those thick chocolate shakes, watch porno, and pretend some little hottie was going to screw him senseless. Maybe the little unlucky redhead at the back of the bus would survive the ordeal.

He flashed a cool grin and enjoyed the air whistling in from the vacant windshield he'd kicked out. The ocean breeze tangled with his straggly dirty blond hair, struggling to stay in the ponytail he'd fastened.

Joy. He realized he actually began to understand what the Guardians called joy.

They didn't have a decent sound system on the purple beast, but it did have an aging CD player mounted and swinging back and forth. It was attached with a red and yellow striped bungee cord wrapped around the oversized rearview mirror stem. Somebody probably had to bring their own music to calm the faint of heart as they drew out that wonderful red honey. Keep the customers calm. Get them to give it up for free like that girl at the prom some seventy years ago.

Now that was a nice night.

He grabbed for another bag in the egg crate at his feet, roared as he felt his fangs come back to life— longer, whiter, and sharper. He sucked the elixir and then swore as his dick elongated another inch, pushing against the steering wheel, causing the bus to swerve and almost topple. He adjusted himself and continued to drive with new focus.

Not yet. Can't crash yet.

It had been an impulse decision to steal the bus. With his man toys of destruction strapped to his back, he'd been cruising overhead, excited about leaving his perch on the bridge, and all of a sudden it was like the Heavens opened. The purple bus was right there below him, ripe and ready for its voyage into the unknown.

He'd barked at the male tech who was gassing up the vehicle and then fled on foot, without Gideon having to lay a finger on him. They didn't have any decent music. Only thing he could find were *Phantom of the Opera* CDs stashed in a hole in the dashboard. He left the little redheaded phlebotomist hiding in the back as he fired up the engine and streaked off towards San Francisco, the gas line still briefly attached. No need for a fill-up today.

Today, we're going to fly.

He could hear her frantically whispering on her cell phone from the bathroom, as if the cardboard walls of the bus would shield her calls for help.

"I agreed to one date. You said the guy was nice. Well, he's gone now this monster has taken the bus. I'm stuck in the back," she was saying. "Don't think he knows I'm here. Please, send someone. I didn't sign up for this."

Gideon smiled. His dick lurched so he slapped it down with another growl. He'd unwittingly found a *professional.* Talk about his lucky day! If she survived, perhaps she could be an evening snack, and God knew he liked to play with his food first. He hadn't had a bite of that for over fifty years. Christ, he'd practically been a priest.

The *Phantom* CD was at max.

"I'll be beside you. To comfort and to guide you."

He had a lot in common with the Phantom, he thought, as he entered the Rainbow Tunnel just north of the bridge. He howled through the open windows and heard the echo of his own voice bounce off the arched tube. It would scare everyone inside the structure, but it made his soul turn to flame. He gained on a family in a green Jeep to his right, the dad giving him the once over, not sure what he was really seeing. The driver slowed down and let Gideon pass.

"Smart fellow," Gideon mumbled.

Coming upon the bridge approach, he saw the silver and white skyline of the City, contrasted with the deep blue Pacific Ocean on both sides, dotted with little white sailboats on the Bay side. He swerved to the slow lane. It was such a clear, sunny morning, well before the fog rolled in. His heart raced, thrilled to capacity, as his face and hands began to glow.

"Careful, little one," he called out to a well-muscled woman in her early thirties, dressed in pink, bicycling toward the City. He watched her perfect form, her shapely body, her heart-shaped ass, and decided not to sideswipe her. Some people were just too beautiful to waste. Remembering his mission, he punched down on the pedal, sending a billow of gray smoke out the back as the bus lurched and picked up speed.

He reached down to the floor and pulled up his Carl Gustav 84 mm rocket launcher. One-handed, he aimed it out through the busted windshield, towards the thick cable equidistant between the two towers, the blue open mouth of the bay visible beyond. Holding the tripod of the loaded weapon along his thigh, he pulled the trigger. It hurt like a son of a bitch. He hadn't been too careful; its vibration took out the strip of metal that used to separate the two windshields. But no matter. The anti-tank projectile preceded his forward movement, hitting the bridge cable dead center, snapping it a few seconds before the bus got there. It also took out a twenty-foot section of railing and part of the roadway. Support cables instantly coiled and waved in the air like snakes after being sprung. One tiny adjustment of the steering wheel to the right, and the monstrous purple bus headed off the bridge through the gaping hole, on its maiden flight.

He wondered if this was how it felt to be in a dirigible, wafting through thin air with only the sound of the wind whistling through the window holes.

Time stood still. He saw the cup glued to the dash filled with shuddering pencils, so he tossed them out the driver's side and watched as they found their own way. He wondered what it would look like, his big purple bus and the pencils and blood flying in the air in free fall. He searched for other objects that might impale him and found none. He wondered if there were any Guardians out there yet, if there would be angelic witnesses to this historic flight. He couldn't wait to hear the rumors.

Except now he would join the ranks of the fallen—a casualty of trying to be so good for way too long.

SB really should have known better. It's not nice to fool Mother Nature.

The bus took a nosedive, headed straight for the choppy waters of the ocean, and all of a sudden, he was covered with the redheaded female who had practically fallen into his lap. She would have been the first to hit, a projectile headed straight through the windshield, but he held her firm little waist and pressed her back to his chest. He could smell her fear and felt the sigh as she lost consciousness.

Lovely.

The impact as he hit the water was shockingly cold, and whitish green, not the deep blue of the bay he had seen when he was watching or sailing through the sky. Shielding his prize with his arms, he rode the bus down like a dagger plunging into the breast of the San

Francisco Bay.

In no time at all, the bus rested on the bottom, touching down as gracefully as a space shuttle landing, first the front and then the rear wheels. He was right. The frame held rigid after all.

And here they were, two would-be lovers under two hundred feet of water. She was light, and no problem for him. He lifted his bride out of their watery sanctuary like a trophy.

Live, my dear. Witness my power. He kissed her plump pink lips and blew air into her lungs, feeling her breasts heave into his chest. His desire flamed.

Holding her firmly, he drilled like a bullet through the water and then punched into the air above, shedding his wet clothes. His once-white wings had now turned black.

So it's true. When you fall, they turn. Even though drenched, his new plumage worked perfectly well, in fact, better than his old ones. They were stiffer and larger as he flapped them and felt their thirst for flight. Their response was more immediate as he flexed and released his massive shoulder muscles connected like cables to his neck.

Holding her tight, he landed on the cliffs at the Marin side overlooking the bridge. He'd pressed her breasts against his bare chest, attempting to keep her heart warm, letting her legs dangle over his thighs. Hoping she was not dead, he was overjoyed to feel her femoral artery pulsing deliciously close to her sex. He let its pumping massage his dick.

He put out the call telepathically and immediately heard the Guardians coming in full force, frantic and screaming. He loved the cross-chatter as they divided up the soon-to-be victims and made quick decisions who to save and who to let go. They were prohibited from allowing themselves to be seen, which Gideon knew was a huge problem for them. He chuckled.

Cars fell into the bay like pebbles as the platform pavement between the north and south towers collapsed, sending a cascading shudder all the way to San Francisco. The surprise destruction caused a twinge of regret for the loss of life. He hadn't intended or thought about that.

The gap between the two towers looked more like a toothless grin without the roadway between them. The connection between Marin and San Francisco was severed, just like the First Nation had found it some thousand years ago, just as the Supreme Being had made it before the touch of man had joined them.

He examined the little redhead, holding her lithe body across his lap. He kissed life into her lungs again, and she stirred, making a mockery of the bra that

SHARON HAMILTON

dared to hide her bursting bosom from him. He would burn that device, but later, after he'd tasted her and savored his crime. His disobedience. She would be his reward for a job chillingly well done.

He'd forgotten how arousing it was to bring them back from the edge of death. It was so completely wicked to play with his food, but the warm glow after having inhaled her essence was making him feel bigger and stronger than ever before. He felt positively ageless. It could almost be called a religious experience—something he'd never expected.

With a quick thought, her clothes disappeared, just as an overcoat, white shirt and black leather pants appeared for him, constraining his wild cock from scaring her. Her peach mounds, accentuated by taut deep red nipples praying to the heavens, begged to be suckled. His large hand clutched and kneaded her left breast while his mouth savored her right, running his tongue and teeth over her as he tasted the flesh of woman, denied him for so long.

She was so sexy in her unconscious state, her mouth open, succulently exhaling her scent all over his face. Her silky skin, far from satisfying the burning in his soul, only made him want more. He nipped a little at her neck, just enough to taste a drop of her red goodness. The taste was sweeter than he'd imagined after all these years. He was instantly hooked, addicted to her. An electric shiver traveled from the cup he made with his tongue to hold the precious drop all the way down to his groin.

No, she wouldn't be his meal. She would be his executioner. He would plunder her gifts and suffer a fate worse than death: eternity in the Underworld. Death's warm arms would embrace him while he commanded his body to do things to her, making her beg for him. His cock thickened at the thought of her screaming his name as he took her over and over again.

He snuck a quick peek at the bridge as she began to stir. The Guardians were flying in all directions, some even colliding, sending white feathers and sparkle dust down into the bay water. He loved hearing their confusion, their ineffectiveness against the slaughter.

Welcome to my world.

He looked down at the naked redhead and smiled. He held her jaw tenderly in the palm of his right hand and tucked her closer to him, safe and warm. He could completely ravish her and spoil the view. But at this second, he was feeling magnanimous, taking his time with her semiconscious state, not hurrying to claim her thoroughly. More thoroughly than she'd ever realize she could be taken.

"Yes, sweet thing. Come back to me," he whispered, blowing warm air into her hairline just in front of her ear. He could hear a slight ticking sound as the little bubbles of her red elixir traveled down the arteries in her neck, pooling at her sex, making her drunk with her own goodness. "I have you now. No one else will ever touch you again." He lingered on the word "touch," which gave him chills.

She arched, responding to the resonance of his voice. One arm cascaded above her head and then rested. The other smoothed over the muscles of his chest, and he felt the pulsing of her systems firing back to life and the sizzle like a blood stream he'd walked into sometime in his past. She snuggled into the warm jacket he'd divined. Her lips lightly grazed his skin, or did they? Her little pink tongue ventured out tentatively as he cradled her like a baby chick. She was unspoiled and stunning in her confusion, her scent overwhelming him. He bridled himself, adjusted his body so his clothed bulges mated with the soft caverns of hers.

He knew it wouldn't last as her consciousness ramped up, beginning with a whirring sound as she tried to return to her normal life. She probably had family, people who would miss her and worry that she was gone. But all that could come later, when she was ready. He was just delaying her, he told himself. Just

GIDEON

taking a little of what he deserved for being such a good and humble servant for so long.

She cuddled closer to him again and sighed.

"Ahh." She held his power in her soft inhale and exhale. He watched her press in to him, felt her heartbeat spike, as she squeezed her knees together, curling them up in his lap and pushing a scent toward him that said she was aroused and fully wet.

Perfect. Live for me. You are my doorway to the other side. I shall worship the ground you walk on.

He looked back at the bridge. A distant clunk caught his attention as a large truck slammed into a line of empty cars and pushed a green Volkswagen over the edge into the precipice. The little splash it made as it hit the Bay was nearly imperceptible. That was the last one. It looked like the Guardians were all busy.

Sucks for you.

A new Guardian came like a jet overhead, crashing into the ocean where the car had fallen. Soon, the little green bug bobbed in the water with someone clinging to the roof. It looked like all had been saved after all. Gideon was glad. He didn't have it in for humans, just other angels. It wouldn't be fair for humans to pay the price for his indiscretions. It wasn't their fault.

Right on cue, his cell phone rang, which surprised

him. The golden case vibrated, as if shaking itself free of the water like a dog.

He expected old SB would have some choice words, although he'd never heard the fellow swear. As Gideon perused the destruction in front of him, he heard sirens and smelled the acrid trace of smoke. Palming her buttocks just enough to elicit another moan from her most pleasurable mouth, he squeezed the nubile young redhead to his chest. This human woman he was going to fuck six ways to Sunday. As the phone continued to ring, he wondered which sin his mentor would be most upset with. Would Gideon even get a chance to explain himself?

Explain himself? *Is there an explanation?* he mused as he flipped open the phone. The bright yellow screen showed the familiar series of ten plus signs across the bar of the display.

His little golden crosses. How orderly and fitting.

Before he could hear the wrath of the Supreme Being, he flipped the phone closed and hurled it several hundred yards and watched his small missile slip into the ocean without a sound.

Wish it were that easy to be rid of him. He scanned the heavens. Nothing seemed to darken the bright light of the sun, but it would be wise not to stay exposed, just in case SB's vengeance took the form of lightning. Gideon still hated fire.

Except in his soul. The realms of Heaven and the angelic beings there hadn't quenched his thirst or healed the wound at his core. He was still partially vampire and had no business being angel.

A square peg in a round hole.

Did they know he lusted for all of them? Lusted for their angelic blood and the gifts they so teasingly stored under semi-see-through white gowns that drove him crazy? Did his mentor know what a liability he was, a spring ready to release his seed throughout the bright perfection that was Heaven?

She stirred, and he lapped the threadlike trickle of blood exiting the puncture wound in her neck. He groaned, slamming his eyes shut, inhaling all her wonderful female scents. He felt her fingers move over his left pectoral muscle. He swirled his own breath over her in a glamour that would erase her memory of the last few minutes. When he opened his eyes, her clear green luminous gaze impaled him as if she was not totally human. If she were fully conscious and aware, she'd feel his hardening manhood pressing for sanctuary between the crack in her behind. He was grateful she didn't move away.

"What happened?" Her pouty pink lips revealed white teeth and a sexy little pink tongue he suddenly wanted wrapped around his cock.

"There was an accident. I rescued you." He

breathed over her face, adding more of his glamour and watched her eyes half close as she arched her spine and sent her lovely breasts up closer to his mouth. Did she want him to kiss them again? He lowered his head until he was an inch from her lips. He put his words inside her mouth. "I am your Guardian angel."

"Angel?"

He smiled and nodded. He was going to ask her if she wanted to call someone, though he would try to dissuade her from that course of action. He just wanted to distract her a little bit to sample some of the things that had been denied him for so long.

But suddenly she looked at his lips, then raised her eyes to his, and sucked him in. He had no choice, but he was surprised she wasn't afraid. He bent and kissed her again and felt her moan into his mouth as if she was giving up her soul. He was captured, stirred nearly to tears.

A cheap San Francisco motel room watching porn wasn't going to be good enough. He decided on another more glorious plan.

A loud rumble interrupted his journey of delving his tongue deep into her, finding hers and playing with it. Supreme Being was calling.

And he wasn't going to answer. Not until he got good and fucked.

CHAPTER 2

"PERSEPHONE HERE TO see you, sir," Cedric addressed Father, who was seated on a raised dais. Two grade-school-aged cherub boys were lounging on the steps at his feet. They were in the midst of a reading lesson. Father's white hair and beard encircled his full, slightly tanned face, like egg white frosting.

"Ah, welcome, Persephone," Father greeted. "Now, boys, you must leave us in private," he boomed to the two young angels. One of them, the shorter one, burst into tears.

Father sighed and drew the boy to his chest, then kissed the top of his head. "Talbot, you must mind the sensitivity." Pushing the boy out in front of him with powerful hands gripping the youngster's shoulders, he spoke, "You will be no good to the human population if you let your feelings get in the way. We must talk about this some time." Father frowned.

"Yes, sir." The boy wiped tears from his cheeks

with the backs of his hands.

"Okay then. Off with both of you. Go downstairs to Mrs. Dickenson. Ask her to find you a treat."

The two little angels' eyes widened as they sprouted small white wings and began to flutter toward the doorway, giggling.

"Wait!" Father called out. Both boys landed immediately with two light taps as their feet hit the ground. "No wings here. If you are going to work with the human population, you have to know how to walk and act like one of them. Your wings are only for emergencies. Mind the enthusiasm, you two."

"Yes, sir," they chimed in unison. They bolted through the doorway. Persephone could hear their whoops and hollers all the way down the stairs. She could not hear footsteps.

Father shook his head, but he smiled. "You remember those days? I love little ones who are so excited, full of life."

"Yes, sir. Although I was turned as a young woman."

"And you were chosen for your enthusiasm." He got up and motioned her to a pair of overstuffed chairs next to a roaring fireplace. Persephone sat, but Father stood, gazing through the stained-glass window overlooking Heaven's playhouse. His hands were clasped behind him as he thought about something that made him frown again.

"Persephone, Gideon has gone missing."

"Gideon, sir?"

"Your first soul."

"Oh! Gideon. I remember him. The tall one who saved the woman from the truck. Very brave. Very handsome." She blushed and ducked her head slightly. "When did he go missing?"

"This morning."

"I've totally lost track of him." Father probably knew she was lying. She'd looked at the bridge every time she was called to assignment there. One day, Father'd caught her trying to bring Gideon a cup of hot tea.

"Yes, well, he's been on special assignment in the human world. And I'm afraid a bit isolated. I may have made a mistake there."

"He used to growl at me every time I saw him in the hallway during his training. A most ungrateful angel, if I may say so myself."

Father chuckled. "Yes, it seems Gideon has become more ungrateful as the years of isolation have gone by. And now he has gone dark."

"Perhaps that was his true nature?" she asked.

"Yes, well he's different than most. He was not *en-*

tirely human."

"*Sir*?"

"You never knew?"

"Knew *what*, sir?"

"Gideon was vampire."

Persephone felt her blood pressure rise. "You mean—?"

"Yes. Turning him was a mistake. He already *was* immortal."

"Oh, goodness. But forgive me if I need to ask, why would he be upset with this?"

"Because you forever altered him. He's no longer a full-blooded vampire. He's now part Guardian. Sort of like emasculating a strong male human. You understand?"

Persephone blushed again and searched for answers in her toes.

"I'm sorry. Perhaps that's not a good analogy," Father whispered.

"No, I understand your meaning perfectly." Her cheeks felt hot, a most disturbing reaction.

"Good."

"Then what is he?" she begged to ask.

Father chuckled. "Very good question. I'm not quite sure we have a name for it. But I call him a hybrid."

"A hybrid? So how does that work?"

"I wasn't sure. That's why he's been at the top of the Golden Gate Bridge for fifty years. I was hoping he'd take to liking it up there all alone. You see, I've built free will into angel DNA. But I don't think a *dark* path, even though he was already vampire, is what he was destined for." Father turned and looked into her eyes. "He denies his light side now."

"Shame. That is truly a shame!"

"No, my dear. I think it brings with it some opportunity to do some housekeeping."

"*Sir*?"

"It's a labyrinth, you know, the circle of life and death, light and dark. Sometimes in a brief snapshot of time, it looks like the dark forces are stronger, looks like a step back. But it winds about, and you never really know where it's going to turn out until the end." He chuckled again and added, "It's like the kudzu of life. It just grows and grows and alters and changes everything in its grasp."

"Well, if you say so, sir. Can't say as I understand completely." She had no idea what kudzu was and was afraid to ask him. She figured it was probably something he'd created and now regretted doing so.

"No? Well then, you understand I don't ever give up on angels. Or humans either."

"Or vampires?"

"Or vampires. I'll bet you never thought they existed."

"No, sir. I thought it was make believe."

"Truth is sometimes stranger than fiction. Trust me on that." Father was gazing out the window again. "I want everyone to have time to choose the right path. This is why I haven't changed him back, although I could have."

"This I know, sir. You'd have been correcting my mistake, otherwise."

Father abruptly turned and faced her again. "It's never a mistake to care about someone *else*. Human, angel, or other being. Never a mistake."

"But it still remains that I made a mistake in turning him. My inexperience. I am *so* sorry, Father."

"So this is what I'm going to do. I'm sending you on a special assignment to find Gideon. And I don't think he'll be expecting to see you. He thinks I'll be coming after him. You see, Persephone, he's been very, very bad."

"Oh dear."

"And I want you to follow him, since you're the one who turned him. But be careful. He is more apt to do something even more unpredictable than before when you saw him in the hallways. Something stronger than growling at you."

"Do you think he will cause me harm?"

"You will be under my special protection. But yes, he may try. Be cautious, but I ask also that you find compassion for him in this difficult time." Father turned back to the window, the colors of the stained glass washing over his face. "He's going to need it."

PERSEPHONE HOVERED OVER Gideon's abandoned post at the top of the north tower. She could still smell his scent as well as the acrid smell of smoke, oil, and fear. Fear did indeed have a scent, she'd learned. This scent was definitely Gideon's.

As she scanned the destruction below, picking up traces of the Guardian messages, she was relieved to discover everyone on the bridge had somehow survived. Cars remained buoyed in the water longer than normal, and a nearby container ship lent a hand with lifeboats. The Coast Guard was busy trolling back and forth, sending divers back into the water to search for additional victims. But she was satisfied no further harm had befallen the good people of Marin and San Francisco or the tourists on the bridge, and that the Guardians were the cause of the save. She was extremely proud.

She touched down on the cool, slippery rust-painted metal, encasing her cellophane-thin wings back in the wing sacs at her shoulder blades with a snap, and watched dying sunlight pour into the waters of the Pacific outside the Golden Gate. She loved this time of day—the blue sky bursting with dark clouds rimmed in light grey, with shards of sunlight filtering through. The bridge itself was truly golden, but she'd always wondered why they painted it rust red, like dried blood.

Looking down, her bare white toes were cold, so she divined a pink hooded jacket and knee-high leather boots that were lined in flannel. Pink flannel with yellow daisies.

There were no cars snaking down below. Twenty-foot barricades with yellow flashing lights blocked off both entrances to the bridge. The empty tollbooths were host to rescue vehicles and police and other unmarked cars, as well as officials walking all over the approach to the bridge. The scenic point on the Marin side was closed to public access but the parking lot was filled with official vehicles. Two tan and green military boats were evaluating the piers at the water's edge. Sea traffic was halted as a debris ship identified, marked with inflatable buoys and retrieved debris. A salvage barge was steaming on its way to pick up large pieces of cable, hunks of car parts and other miscellaneous debris.

It was eerie not to have the sounds of motors rev-
ving, rap music blaring or air brakes being applied. A
couple of Caltrans trucks started up near the bridge
office and took off towards the City.

She understood how lonely it must have been for
Gideon, that strange angel she had turned years ago.
She had been proud of the turning, her first. Gideon
was the sort of man she was always afraid of—dark and
brooding—but non-violent. That fateful day he lay
dying, sacrificing himself to save the young girl from
the large delivery truck. With nearly supernatural
strength, probably because he was in love with the girl,
he tossed her body out of harm's way like she was a rag
doll. But he'd assembled super-human strength and
she landed poorly, her neck at an odd angle.

It broke her heart to see how he'd been so focused
on getting her to safety, he misjudged the speed of the
truck, which hit him with its enormous grill, and
dragged poor Gideon for yards, leaving parts of him all
over the roadway. Gideon screamed and slithered out
from under the enormous cab of the truck. Beginning
to bruise and covered in blood, he wept in anguish
over the sight of the girl's nude lifeless body in a bed of
flowers at the side of the road. Persephone briefly
wondered why the woman was naked, but put that

thought out of her mind. She could see he still cared about her welfare, even as his own life was being extinguished.

He looked so weak. Remarkably, he attempted to stand but fell back, unconscious. Persephone deduced he was not only in great physical torment, but he grieved for the girl. And that's exactly when she decided to save him. He deserved his wings. She had thought Father would be more pleased. It was a shame to let such a hero die.

Persephone thought he might be finally dead, but as she approached, she saw he was just barely alive. She bent over his white face, straining from the obvious pain and fear that his life was ending. She heard him mumble something and then repeat it.

"Tell me, brave hero. What is your wish?" she spoke to him, allowing him to visually see her, while using some of her dust to dampen his pain. It fell in sparkles around his handsome face. Persephone's heart was dancing along with the choirs in Heaven in the background.

"Let me catch my breath a minute. I'll be fine," he said, his voice raspy with a disturbingly deep rumble.

It warmed her heart to hear this. "Silly. You are a true hero. Protecting the innocent and then not even thinking about yourself."

Gideon squirmed and made a sour face.

She wasn't expecting him to know what was coming next, that she could save him. "I'm going to match your good deed with one of my own. You'll see."

Gideon looked up at her with horror in his eyes.

"Who the fuck—"

"Shhh, shhhh. Don't use any more of your strength." She pulled aside his ragged shirt, seeing the ribs poking through his chiseled chest. With the puddle of blood now forming around her knees as she straddled his hips, she knew the skin covering his back was shredded and nearly gone. The ragged edge of his right humerus bone protruded through his well-developed bicep. She expected he'd go into shock any second, so she worked quickly, placing a hand over the gaping chest wound, which glowed yellow, then white. She gripped his upper arm and applied the same healing to it and felt the bones align, the connective tissues wrapping themselves around for protection, and then the healing of his deep flesh wound and bicep muscle beneath. She admired the smooth surface of his enormous shoulders and arms.

And then she lifted him and brought him with her to Heaven.

There had been a celebration that day. Her first soul. And he was a big specimen, although she didn't dare look on him as a man. He was healed in perfect form and an angel now. On the path to becoming Guardian. He would now live forever, to be able to protect humans. Forever saved and free from the bonds and limitations of an earthly body.

Persephone had done well, or so she thought until the conversation this afternoon with Father. Now storm clouds gathered, dark and dangerous.

So what happened? The angel never thanked her like others would do in subsequent years. In fact, he harbored anger toward her, so she avoided him whenever they ran into each other in the teaching center. He was given some private instruction, as he didn't mix well with some of the others, and actually scared more than a few, especially the redheaded Guardians he seemed to be most angry at. Probably because of the redheaded girl he couldn't save, she thought.

So this had been his kingdom then, his place of refuge, she thought as she looked over the chilly bay, wondering why Father made him a Watcher and not a full-fledged Guardian. Gideon seemed to be a man of action, not someone who liked to watch at the sidelines. Perhaps Father's miscalculation, along with her huge initial mistake in turning him, sealed poor Gideon's fate.

Strange.

A can of Red Bull stood alone on top of the tower, defying the wind. Well, it was time to visit Gideon, and perhaps she would bring him his favorite drink as an introduction. It was time to save him again!

Will he recognize me?

CHAPTER 3

HER PHEROMONES WERE blazing. The little redhead was light as he transported her through the cool air high above the green hills north of Marin County. She nearly floated in his arms. She turned and placed her cheek against his chest, bracing against the wind. Her cheek warmed his breast and caused him to inhale. How he wanted to pull back her hair and drink from her. She surprised him by grazing her lips across the smooth flesh of his pecs. She teasingly missed a nipple, generating a soft moan from deep inside his chest.

"My Guardian," she whispered, kissing his breast afterward which sent a vibration all the way to his cock. "Here I thought I'd be ended by some deranged monster. But even *I* have a Guardian!"

It was an odd comment, but he suspected she suffered from low self-esteem, so dismissed his reservations. "Yes." He smiled down at her and saw her blush. "How do you feel?"

She scanned his face, touched his cheek with her tiny fingers, ending with her forefinger tracing over his bottom lip. She took in a deep breath. "Grateful."

He nearly dropped her he had gone so rigid. Now he wondered if he'd be able to make the trip home without a mishap of some kind. He'd never fucked while flying before, but perhaps today was the day…

"You need to contact home, let people know you're all right?" he asked as the wind whooshed through his hair. He cupped her, sheltering her from the cold.

Her smile was as wicked as he'd seen on his vamp mentor. "I'm all alone right now. With you."

The rumble from a distant bolt of lightning made him shiver. He tore his gaze away from her and concentrated on the trip, urgent to get her to his bedroom.

"Am—am I flying?" she asked him. Her green eyes beckoned the truth.

"Yes. See my beautiful wings?" He allowed his shoulders to tense, hitching his powerful dark wings up overhead, making a flapping noise as a special sound effect just for her. She buried her head in his chest.

She wasn't nervous, being carried through the clouds as he'd worried she would be. She snuggled into the embrace of their shared warmth.

He wondered if he could still trace to speed their journey. He'd not tried it for several years.

The sky thundered, and the sunny morning became dark and wintery. He decided not to risk harming the little human woman, so continued his flight north. It wouldn't be long now.

Who knew something so beautiful could rise from the ashes of this near-tragedy? Could survive just because of the protection of his arms. He understood the sheer terror she must have experienced as the bus plunged into the bay, just before the water turned black. And yet, she survived! He'd saved her!

Her fingertips explored the groove between his enormous muscles, lacing down the smooth valley of his midsection. As they began to descend, he dropped her knees and pulled her against him, holding her waist and allowing her to slip just slightly, over his erection. She flung her arms around his neck, encircling his hips with her thighs.

He was thrilled.

They hit ground softly, and she hesitantly unwrapped. The landing had enough of a jolt so that the delicious feel of his cock rubbing against her core brought him ecstasy. Her thighs grazed his. She seemed to be in no hurry, and he closed his eyes and savored the warmth between them like two carefully crafted pieces of a puzzle. Gideon licked his lips, and inhaled her scent. Standing on her own, but solidly pressed against his body, she blushed, braced herself, stepped back, gazing down at her bare feet, and took a deep breath. Her naked beauty seemed to bring a hush to the whole universe. Gideon applied his fingers just under her jaw, tipping her face to look up at him. His other hand reached down and completely covered and squeezed the left cheek of her rear, and then released her with a pat. She was emboldened, pulling his face down to hers, intent on stealing a kiss from him. His mouth watered as he arched down so slowly, resisting her pulls, making her work harder while judging and calculating her strength and vitality. He hovered unhurriedly closer and closer to her hungry mouth. She tugged down on his thick neck and the back of his head. It made him chuckle how strong the little waif was. Her fingers squeezed the wet, curly shoulder-length hair at the back of his head, her eyes tenaciously focused on the angle of his mouth.

At last his lips melted over hers, quenching his thirst for her but creating an even greater need. Their tongues found each other and explored, lips sucking, giving and receiving the breath of each other's passion. The feeling of her bare breasts against his chest started an electric buzz that vibrated her lithe body. His already rock-hard cock stiffened further and pressed against her abdomen. She removed one hand from his neck, heading down to touch him there, when he stopped her and kissed the palm of her hand, then licked her wrist. He showed her his longer-than-normal canines, and her brow furled in a frown.

He whispered in her ear, "I would never hurt you. Never."

She melted in to him in response and appeared to accept him in his hybrid form. He marveled at her courage, or perhaps it was her previous experience.

No matter. I am at last a Guardian. I have saved a human woman!

Another loud thunderclap punctuated the air. "Come. We need to go inside," Gideon said, motioning to the large oak door entrance to his estate. Spurred on by her acceptance, he decided to try out his newly rediscovered skills, and was able to bring her through the door by *tracing* them through.

She squealed in delight.

He led her through a dark, carved, wooden archway twice her height into the grand foyer and living room beyond. Gideon viewed his vineyard, bringing her to the arched picture windows off the living room. The leaves were like her flesh, blushing burgundy and pale apricot. The darker the clouds became, the brighter the foliage appeared.

He hadn't left her side, but kept them joined along

one long leg line, one arm around her waist. When they arrived at the windows overlooking the view, he stood behind her. With hands on her hips, he ground his pelvis to her backside and kissed her just under her right ear. He pressed his canines to her flesh, claiming her, commanding she obey his every desire with his glamour.

She placed her palms above his hands and moved them to her breasts and squeezed him over them.

"Yes," he said.

Her submission was sweet as she angled her head, exposing her neck again to him, begging him to take what she somehow knew he wanted. Was she telepathic? His writhing tongue took a long, languid stroke against her carotid artery, and then he inhaled and bit down. He felt her core react, as spasms of a sharp, powerful orgasm overcame her. She rocked back and forth while his arms held her close to his heat. He bit down on her neck again, which drove her wild.

He felt her fear when he ended his feeding, perhaps not being properly chaste and taking too much of her. But he'd not been able to totally control his urge. The more he drank, the more he wanted of her. His lack of female companionship had obviously left him famished and overcome with his vampiric side left dormant and neglected for so long.

She tilted forward slightly, pressing against his desire, asking to be taken. But he held himself back and enjoyed the feel of the friction against his throbbing member.

He finished his lovemaking drink with a lick to her bruised neck, and then he ended with a pert kiss.

"You are luscious, my dear." The hot words lingered heavy between them. "I've... I've never..."

She quickly turned, facing him and placing her palm against his mouth just after his tongue swiped his bottom lip to lap up the droplet of her blood left there. "Shhh. Don't say anything. I don't want to know anything. I just want to feel this."

Again, she'd surprised him, and he gave her back an incredulous smile. But behind it, he grew cautious as if some distant alarm had struck.

Is this all too easy?

But he put it out of his mind. "Come." He allowed his voice to wash over her, hoping to enhance her erotic thoughts. She appeared to resist his glamour.

"What do I call you?" she asked.

"Thought you didn't want to talk," he said as he led her by the hand up the white marble stairway like taking her through the Pearly Gates themselves.

"You don't want me to call out your name? How perfectly odd. Most males enjoy me screaming their names to the Heavens. As an angel, don't you find it so?" She made a mock frown and stopped.

"You first. What do I call you?" he asked.

"Ashley." Her name floated in slow motion over his face, producing a small electric current traveling down his spine. Her luminous green eyes glowed, sending heat straight to his chest.

"That's nice. I love the name Ashley."

"Now you."

"Lover. Call me Guardian lover," he said as he swept her into his arms again. "But if it's all the same to you," he whispered in her ear, "let me see it in your eyes and taste it in your blood." He was going to suggest she scream it telepathically but decided not to complicate something that was already going very nicely for him. Why spoil it?

She leaned back, nearly fainting, but he lifted her under the arms and knees and carried her up the remaining steps, kicking open the gothic bedroom double doors like breaking into a cathedral.

At the sight of the bedroom, she held her breath. The light brown marble fireplace with white veins throughout the smooth stone was engulfed in flame he caused, bringing instant warmth to the room. The fireplace was large enough for her to stand in. A set of French doors were to the right, opening to a tile-floored balcony that stretched wide, overlooking the colored hills of the vineyard. Wrought iron handrails with heart-shaped designs framed the outdoors, matching the drapery rods inside the room, dripping with sheer silks and satin materials wafting in the breeze. There was the familiar smell of cinnamon and myrrh, as well as the ancient untraceable scents of his people.

Directly ahead, he carried her with slow, sleek movements from his vampiric predator side, to lay her across his hand-carved four-poster bed with raised two-step platform beneath. A burgundy velvet coverlet stitched with designs in gold and silver thread covered the massive bed, dipping all the way and spilling to the floor. As if she were a delicate piece of porcelain, he nestled her there in a sitting position at the edge of the bed and grazed her calves with his fingertips, following from her knees to her ankles and then feet, pressing them gently to the floor. His large hands slightly squeezed the balls of her feet, and he felt a warm tingle travel all the way up her spine. He knelt before her, put his hands together, and bowed his head.

She slid off the bed and straddled his thighs, encased in black leather pants. She lazily sifted the long hair at the back of his neck, her breasts at the level of his mouth, pressing one knotted nipple to his lips.

Her head arched backward as his tongue tasted, pulled, and his fangs nipped her. He felt her core spasm again. Her fingers trailed behind his ears and under his jawline as she drew his chin up and studied his eyes. The green glow coming from hers pulled things from inside his soul he suddenly couldn't help but share with her.

"I worship the ground you walk on," he said without warning, surprising himself. He had never uttered these words before.

"I am the one who should worship you," she whispered. "Your perfect body, your strength. Because of you, I am here to enjoy this afternoon." She covered his wet mouth with hers. Gideon's huge boner was in danger of exploding as he pushed up against her and growled. Her pulse quickened and her eyes briefly widened. She was panting for air again, nearly at the edge of an orgasm already, and he wasn't even inside her. Gideon knew at that moment this woman was made for pleasure.

"How did you find me? How did you recognize I needed saving?" she asked, looking from one eye to the other. When her gaze turned to his chest, he felt his skin tingle.

He hesitated with the answer for just a second. A thunderclap outside distracted him.

"Uh, I got vibrations. I felt your fear when he scared off the other tech and you were alone with him. When he stole the bus."

She arched backwards at first, then straightened and examined his expression again. He felt like she was pulling truth from him. Saying things he couldn't stop from saying.

"Where were you?" Even her wrinkled brow was intoxicating.

"At... at... at the truck stop where your coworker was gassing up." He reached up to kiss her again, but she drew back. Gideon felt the gentle shift in energy at that very moment. She scrambled to her feet and walked to the center of the room. He followed her but kept a wary distance. Darkness was seeping into his mood.

"How did you follow the bus?"

"I flew. I can fly, as you know."

"Why didn't you stop the bus from going off the edge? If you are a Guardian angel, why didn't you stop the bus, save the bridge, and those people I watched fall into the bay?"

He paused, unsure how to answer her.

"I saved *you* instead."

"But you let all those people die!"

"It... it wasn't my job. Other angels came to save

them all. It's hard to explain."

The mood had definitely shifted. She impaled him square in the eyes. "Try harder."

CHAPTER 4

*O*F ALL THE *fornicating Greek gods in Heaven and the Underworld! Have you never spoken to a woman before?*

It had all been going so nicely. He was fully aroused on that rock overlooking the bay. Why did he let her see the little cars kerplunking into the cold water?

You complete idiot! Have you forgotten how to be the powerful vampire you used to be? He loved chasing young girls and hearing their screams just before he took their life. His gift was to leave them with an orgasm ten times as strong as any they had experienced before. If they died, they died in bliss. If he happened to take a life because their bodies couldn't handle his need, at least they'd invited him in at the end. The blood was good, laced with passion, fresh fruit of a life snuffed out at its peak, before hateful doubting thoughts became resident in their souls.

And he hadn't wanted to end her life, just enjoy her

thoroughly. He was good at it. *Really* good at it! Ending her life was now something he wanted to avoid at all costs, perhaps evidence that he had adopted some of the angel qualities bestowed upon him without his permission. He was a vampire still, but a vampire with a conscience. A vampire with wings!

But that was before Gideon's "reclamation," as they called it in Heaven. Perhaps some of his other talents were stripped from him, although his blood lust never waned. His ultimate death was still a mystery to him, but waking up as an angel practically sent him over the edge of sanity.

Some fucking reclamation. He still wanted to dip his cock in the folds of their angel pussies and sink his fangs into their heavenly blood. In Heaven, nubile angelic girls had kept him achingly uncomfortable and had surrounded him without mercy. Did they not realize the pain and agony they caused him, their sweet smiles requiring his inner restraint to the point of excruciating pain? He'd exercised his palm so much he nearly had calluses, as the human joke went.

He'd resisted the temptation for years. Stuck on top of the north fucking tower at the Golden Gate Bridge. Freezing his butt off. Watching. Watching for jumpers so he could telegraph a quick memo to the Guardians. Eternity as a Watcher. Removed from everyone except his one angel buddy, Francis.

So today he resisted his Guardian nature and embraced another path, perhaps to a dark angel, judged by his acts like he'd walked through a car wash. White wings to black. Hungry for sex and no desire to hold himself in check. Big fucking deal he didn't try to save all the people on the bridge. The Guardians didn't save everyone who wanted to jump, either. In fact, and just for sport, he'd purposely delayed some transmissions to make the little white "moths" as he liked to call them, have to work up a sweat. He liked the way they smelled when they sweat. It made him horny. Even with all that, they still managed to save everyone. No harm, no foul.

Fuck it.

She had gentled him, not that she knew that. He was going to take what he felt he was owed, had been owed for all those years, but she touched him and that made all the difference. He couldn't take her forcibly. Something ancient rose up and he contracted a sudden case of being a gentleman, worse than an STD followed by conscience.

He hadn't spent any time at all choosing her. How in Hades was he going to convince her he did? He could never tell her he saved her life only because of her blood, her red hair and the way her turquoise

Blood Bank tee shirt stretched over her bulbous breasts before he had willed it all away, along with that horrible contraption called a brassiere. It drove him crazy as he watched her breathe, saw the effect of blood pumping in veins and arteries just under her flawless creamy skin's surface. He'd even considered perhaps Supreme Being wouldn't mind if he fucked between her breasts. He didn't see that rule written anywhere, and it certainly wasn't in the Bible, a boring tome he'd had to memorize frontward *and* backward. The only good thing about Bible study was the young peach-skinned Guardian who taught it. She also liked to take bubble baths and pleasure herself as he spied on her with his stolen telescope.

So SB is angry with me. What else is new? But now there was this girl with many surprise gifts he wanted to experience. And she was looking up at him with doubt all over her face. Why wasn't she afraid of him? Didn't she know he could fly, liked to bite, and wanted to keep her naked and chained to his bed for a couple of weeks at least? How could she give up the best sex of her lifetime for a few stupid answers? About those few pathetic strangers who just happened to be in the wrong place at the wrong time? End of story.

Like her?

No. Something was different about her. He knew it

from the first drop of her blood he tasted. Something sacred was growing, as much as he wanted to track it down and kill it. Something was altering—had altered—his universe, and it would forever be different.

Maybe if he just fucked her, all these doubts would disappear. The room had been mentally set for her. The fireplace, the opened windows, and the silky curtains he knew she would want to wrap her pink body in so he could shred them and get to her flesh. He wanted to feel the soft red velvet on his knees as he pleasured and plundered her gifts, as he made her cry out for him, call him by his real name. Yeah, he could get her to do that, and then maybe he'd be satisfied. Then he'd let them yank him home for his punishment. How long would he last before he started going through the delicate little pink flowers of Heaven's angels? How many of them could he take before he got caught again? And then where would he go? The Underworld was sounding pretty damn good right about now.

She bit his nipple. It fucking hurt. That little minx was now getting on his nerves. So much for small talk.

"I want an answer, you, you with no name." Her scowl was adorable. Evil thoughts raced through him, all the things he could do to her to get even. He saw her tied up, trussed like a turkey, her luscious ass hanging out for him to suckle from underneath as he raised and lowered her body onto his face. He'd make her come so many times just the brush of his sandpaper tongue on her nether lips would cause her to squeeze out her own juices and moan in the agony of it. He'd lap that tight little pussy, maybe bite her a little there, draw some blood, and feel the vibration in her core that begged for him as she struggled and said *no.* It was way more fun that way, he told himself, when they were confused and then finally surrendered gladly to him.

But one glance at her lips and he knew he'd have to work harder with the glamour in order to get them on his cock without biting him.

He checked his nipple and saw the one-inch drip of blood she'd caused. It was getting swollen. Her eyes held no compassion for his pain, his humiliation.

Little twat. You are practically dead.

"Have you no fear of me, human?" He was curious, after all. Even detached.

"Me? Afraid of you?" She raised her eyebrows and smiled, licking those distracting deep rose-colored lips that now began to form an "O" that would look so nice on… "You want something I have," she whispered as she leaned in to him. The warm vibration of her words danced across his face and tickled his ears. He sucked in air. "I'll give you what you want, if you promise to give me what I want."

She was the biggest tease he'd ever met. She was torturing him with the promise of sex he knew would be outstanding. His manly body part was cheering with pompoms and a whole fuckin' brass band.

"Conditional sex, is it? You're trying to drive a hard bargain," he barked, trying to play down how fun he thought all this was.

"I don't have to try. You know you want me, right? Why not surrender to your urge? So much easier that way, angel. Then you could have me all night long."

Bingo. He loved females who bargained, and it was a good deal, too! The smell of her arousal was still on her. He was back, just like he'd been all those years ago, back and ready to be his preangel being, *finally*! Was she saying she didn't mind bad boys? Was that what he was now? Maybe she just needed a clarification. Maybe it was okay he let all those people die. And then his conscience began to work overtime; his angel side crept in. Was this wise?

Who the fuck is she?

As if she was going to answer him, she inhaled and stepped closer, "I'm saying it one more time, angel. You want me? I need something in return from you. This is the price of my complete surrender."

She leaned back, her lids half covering her eyes.

Very slowly she turned and climbed up on his bed, so that he could get a good look at her backside, and the lips of her peach hanging wet and quivering between her legs.

This is so unfair.

His cock was ready to go. No problem, man, it transmitted to him. It was marching to her tune, suddenly feeling naked and needing the warm sheath she was offering. It had tasted her channel in anticipation, seeking to ram itself to oblivion like an errant body part with its own brain.

With her knees spread apart, she lowered her chest to the bed and, with one hand, rubbed her pussy up and down the crack, her sultry green eyes following his expression from the shadows at the head of his bed.

On my bed. Defiling my bed.

But he'd brought her here after all for that very purpose. He was planning to do worse. Now if he took her and then lost her, he would never be able to sleep again on this bed. Gideon fisted his hands at his sides. Things never used to be so complicated! He was caught. He knew now what it meant to give up a kingdom for a piece of ass, something he'd never been able to understand.

Her right forefinger called him with a little curling motion and then plunged into her folds.

I am lost.

CHAPTER 5

GIDEON APPROACHED HER glistening, ripe sex. He tried to look into her eyes, but he was transfixed with the perfectly formed oval of her peach and the gaping slit right down the middle of it. Those two fingers were pushing in and out, sending her scent to envelop him, raising alarms and buzzers all over his body. Her muscles sucked in those digits, but over the noises of her juicy sex, he could hear her ragged breathing and then the moan she made into his plush red bedspread. He was beside himself with need.

He leapt to the bed, placing his knees outside hers and realized he hadn't removed his leather pants. Closing his eyes, he willed them away and felt his huge cock spring forward, bouncing off her right butt cheek. Like it had a mind of its own, the red, velvet tip aimed for her core. He ripped her fingers out, and she threw her head back and laughed with glee. He gripped her waist with his right hand and with his left, spread her lips so he could plunge in.

"No!" she said at first as she began to tense up but then whispered, "Oh, please. Yes," as he filled her. Remarkably, she only groaned. She didn't ask those stupid questions; she let him have her hard.

Now this is more like it. He loved it when they said no but meant yes. And God, she was so tight he was practically creaming already. Even though forced to the hilt, he wanted more. She did, too, as she raised herself up and pressed her backside onto his lap, forcing hard against him so he could penetrate deep. He pumped her like it was his first time. His long wait was over.

But all of a sudden it hit him. What was it she did want? He hadn't agreed to answer any of her questions, and yet, by his actions, he was bound to her just as if he had given her his oath. Is this how she understood it, too?

Oh, this one was wicked. He considered stopping.

No fucking way. It wasn't just that he didn't want to stop. He *couldn't.*

"Harder. Fuck me harder!" she demanded as she turned and sweetly smiled at him, her green eyes half-lidded, egging him on. But then they went all golden and liquidy, like molten metal, unlike anything he'd ever seen.

She screamed, and the whole house shook. He

thought something was wrong for a minute, but then her little ass began to vibrate, and a golden light poured all over his glistening shaft as he pumped her. Her muscles clamped down hard like he'd been bitten and, with her vibrating sex, she milked him, taking every drop of his seed. He unloaded such a wad, it felt like not only his sac, but both his legs had been drained.

A fleeting thought about him losing his pecker forever inside this woman was tempered by the sight of his rod, still rock hard, fat, and ready for more. And try as he might, he could not stop.

She raised her right knee, exposing her belly to him. He slipped her leg over his shoulder as he slid into her deeper at cross-angles. He liked that position, could see her boobs jiggle and shake as he pumped her. And they were just the right size: amply spilling over his large fingers as he squeezed them. She nailed him with her liquid eyes, as the red hair on her forehead got damp and pasted down in dark auburn curls. Her lips made a delicate O, mimicking the button of her ass. She arched backward and sank into the bed, while he watched her eyes tear up, her knee still over his shoulder.

She had already come once, but he could see she was beginning a large steady ascent to another climax, and briefly he worried about whether or not his house would survive the sonic explosion. And he was headed right alongside her, with no signs of going limp.

She suddenly grabbed the long tendrils of his hair and pulled his face to hers. She sucked his lips and pricked her tongue on his fangs and poured her own blood into his mouth. Fueled with the warm burn that slid all the way down his spine from the hot taste of her blood, he smelled the pulsing artery in her neck, drew his teeth over it, and sank in.

His cock lurched, elongated, and deliciously rammed into her soft tunnel seeking its own plunder. She moaned as she rose up into him, giving him her neck fully.

"Oh, God. I knew it. I knew it," she said breathlessly.

Knew what? Bugger it. Let's get this done, and then I have a host of questions for you, my dear.

"I want to taste you too," she whispered.

He stopped for a second, her blood on his lips as he looked into her golden eyes, now turning ruby red. She licked her own blood from his mouth, and smiled.

"You are vampire?" he asked. "You cannot be purely human."

She fell back with a giggle. He was just about to come. He didn't want her giggling when he did. But her sex was vibrating while she was giggling, and he shot her full of warm cum and discovered he loved it. He felt a tickling in his chest and realized he had been chuckling, too. It was kind of funny, fucking this little vixen, who thought he was a Guardian angel, and she thought it was funny he wondered if she was a vampire. Well, he could see from her teeth she was not. Not a white fang in sight. Teeth not made for ripping and tearing flesh, like his.

Vegetarian. He could taste the tofu and green salads. All those heavy workouts so she would have the muscled abs he was staring at, the thighs that made it so she could crack walnuts between her knees.

Who knew sex could be so fun, so outrageous, so freeing? So incredibly exciting and different. Unlike sex he'd remembered. He could seriously do this 24/7 for weeks on end. Never had he felt this way before. Although he'd been the one to save her, he'd been liberated as well. He felt fantastic.

"God, where have you been all my life?" he groaned as he stared up at the ceiling, suddenly remembering he had covered it in mirrors just last week. It was that hot dream he had that made him do it. Did he know she was coming to him?

Yeah, she was coming all right. The scent of her sex would permeate the air for a week. And if he could convince her to be bound with handcuffs, well then, he could do this several times a day.

Naked and shackled in my bed. He looked at the leather straps looming over the headboard. Had she noticed?

She raised her head, found his breast again and squarely bit him on his left nipple. This time it hurt. A lot.

He jerked back. "Ow."

Her mouth was covered in his blood. She ran her tongue over her lower lip and smiled again. "More," she cooed.

Damn, what is happening?

He had to be careful she didn't take too much of his blood, or it would alter her permanently. He tried to hold her head back as she lunged for his tit again, but she was clearly stronger than he thought.

Now this was scary.

She drank until a huge red welt developed outside her lip line, and he knew she had inflicted a large, serious wound. She'd probably had a full cup of his blood. What would his blood do to her?

He didn't have to wait more than about a minute. She drew his cock farther inside and levitated about a foot off the bed, the full weight of his body crushing down on hers as she took him with her. He was going to use his feet as anchors, but instead unfurled his wings with a loud flap like a canvas sail catching the wind.

Her eyes widened as she lifted her fingers and ran them down his wings on both sides, which caused him to shudder at the pure pleasure of her delicate touch. Definitely the first time this had happened to him. He'd always kept his white wings encased in the wing sac covering his shoulder blades. These black ones gave him virile adrenaline, maleness he had never felt before. He drilled her, pumping her so fast with his stiff, fat cock her eyes fluttered back in her skull and he thought she nearly passed out.

But then she arched up, and as if some inner power took hold, her skin began to glow while her eyes turned dark blue, like the color of the sky just before sunset. With a few long, careful strokes, they came together. She was a sheer force of nature. The whole universe folded into her chest as she looked at him with the wisdom of the ages and enough fire to consume all of history. Her spasms wrung the magic out of her, and he could feel her orgasm coating his member, which was spurting like a severed artery. Hot cum shot into her body, washing her insides with such force he could feel the backlash. She closed her eyes and moaned, her muscles massaging him.

Then they melted together, became boneless, sinking back onto the bed.

He'd never been compelled to kiss a woman after sex or tell her she was great. Just wasn't part of his DNA. He wasn't a schoolboy with his first crush. But man, this coupling was amazing, and he had the feeling it would only get better. He wanted to ask her what else she could do. He suddenly wanted to try it all.

So Gideon kissed her as she raised her arms and let her fingers sift through the silver embroidery of the velvet coverlet. He climbed her body and touched her with his thighs, his abs, his chest; he pinned her hands above her head and pressed her arms with his.

"Baby, that was... incredible." He winced internally, dipped his face in the warm wet spot above her shoulder just under her ear. He licked her wounds, leaving some on his tongue to share with her. She was hungry for it.

"We have to be careful with that, you know," he whispered.

"But I don't want to be careful."

Her eyes had gone green again, and with her red hair and peach-toned body splayed out all over his bed, she looked like a forest nymph he'd tracked and dragged home.

For the first time ever, Gideon didn't want to move.

"What was that?" she asked.

"Honey, I don't know. I've... I didn't want it to end. Never felt like that before."

"We have some chemistry, huh?" She smiled wide, and he loved her straight bright white teeth. Normally fangs turned him on, but he liked her top row of perfect teeth.

"So, does this happen every time you have sex?" he had to ask.

"No, this has never happened before to me. You are special."

He didn't believe her. Her answer seemed somehow canned.

She sat up, leaned over, and touched his wound.

"Does this hurt?"

"No," he lied.

"It looks like it hurts." She placed her palm against the raw flesh, and a golden light shone out from under her hand. He felt the heat, but it did not burn him. When she removed her palm, his chest was completely healed. She looked as surprised as he was with the change.

"How did you do that? You have healing powers?"

"I didn't think I did."

"Yes, you do!" he said, pointing to his healed chest. "I would heal on my own, but what you have done, it's a miracle. I've never seen this before. Truly a miracle."

She put her palm against her lips and giggled.

All he could think of was that he wanted her to bite him again, this time on the other side.

CHAPTER 6

G IDEON HAD LEARNED to push his body to stay awake for days at a time. He'd done it for so long he wasn't sure he could even sleep. And now, after his encounter with this beautiful fantasy lady, he was flooded with questions that had no answers. His mind was on overdrive trying to comprehend the reality of who she was, or more importantly, *what* she was. He wondered if he should feel afraid of her for some reason, and after weighing it, decided not to.

As he lay back, her young body warming his left side as she slumbered in a near-coma, he pondered all the possibilities. He would let her rest after the ordeal in the bay and their lovemaking. It felt good to have a companion after so many lonely years by himself without any intimacy. He'd been starved for it. Perhaps because of that he hadn't noticed the odd things about her.

He knew she had special powers, but he did not

think she was immortal like he was. Nevertheless, he had to find out her story.

He thought about his life atop the bridge. One day blended into another, adding up to a string of fifty years of unremarkable days watching the world go by. At least part of the world. He couldn't recall ever sleeping.

Maybe I took catnaps and was so bored I've forgotten?

But try as he might, he could not remember ever falling into a deep restful sleep. Or waking up with a start. Or dreaming. And yet now he felt like he could sleep, finally sleep, if he wanted to. Perhaps that was part of the dark angel nature he'd gained in the turning.

Thinking on it further, Gideon felt it was the dreaming part that he missed the most from his mortal life. As a young man, he had visions of women he intended to bed, of islands he wanted to be marooned on with a woman who wore little or no clothing. Her perfect body ripe for him to see any time he wanted, opening up to him, not making him pay, not like the good girls he had to beg for sexual favors. He wanted someone who loved him for who he was. For the sexual animal he was. Girls who wouldn't judge his overripe libido.

He could barely remember those days before he became vampire, before he became an angel. He'd followed a destiny that now made sense, he mused as he looked over the sleeping form of his lover. She was cuddled against his bare chest, absorbing his strength and passion even as she slept. He felt tenderness toward this little nymph he had not experienced in years and, for the first time in his life, he knew he was on the right path. He belonged again in the land of the undead, as well as the living. Would he be able to take her with him when he was invited to the gates of the Underworld? Would the Director approve without having to sample the goods?

He finally drifted off to sleep and suddenly woke up on his father's farm in Central Oregon. He felt the damp, musty heat in the air while the wheat was growing and heard the sound of wind whistling through eucalyptus trees on its way to the ocean. He'd heard stories about his ancestors who fought in the Civil War, the ones who came out and homesteaded the farm so they could live a life of freedom and abundance.

However, it had been a struggle living on the farm. There was never enough money. The farm was always in danger, and with it, their entire lives. Didn't stop him from lying out on warm summer days and pretending he was the king of everything. Those were magical days when he thought such a thing were possible, when he believed he could help his parents, his brothers and sisters, his grandparents, so they could all live in some gigantic house and not have to work so hard to achieve so little. He wished for golden days idyllically spent harvesting vegetables in the garden and drinking too much of Farmer Spencer's apple brandy he secretly made in the shed behind the big house during prohibition. He and little Jessica Spencer had sold her dad's brandy at the market run by old man Boone, a man who liked to brag that Daniel Boone was his cousin.

But in the end, they'd lost the farm and moved to a smaller plot of land they leased from an older childless black family who raised ducks for the fancy restaurants in Portland and Seattle. Papa Cletis, as he started calling him, taught him about playing cards, and what to say to the ladies, even bought him his first whore, a young scared-to-death black girl named Annabelle. He knew it was her first time too, and that somehow made it all right.

But it wasn't. It really wasn't. He began to wake up, and then forced himself back into the pleasant slumber. He needed to see his old life again, something he hadn't visited for a very long time.

Maybe my old life was the dream.

He went deeply back under. That summer he'd saved up enough money doing chores for neighbors to buy another session with Annabelle, who used to sneak out back on balmy summer evenings and show him what she'd learned from the customers and the other more experienced girls. That was for free. He wanted to do it all proper-like, walk to the front desk and ask for her with a wad of cash burning a hole in his pocket.

They snickered at him, but he got Annabelle one last time in a room all to themselves, where they could experiment all night long, and even got a fireplace and fresh sheets.

She stopped sneaking out to him, and then one day Cletis told him she moved away. Some guy with a big, fancy car bought her, and she left to go work at his house in Chicago, clear across the country. He hoped she was safe and had a good life after all. She was a good person. She deserved as much.

Cletis and his wife lost their farm in a fast-paced game of poker, and just like that, both families were displaced. Over the next few years, his family moved no less than seven times. His grandparents died, his father took to drinking and staring out the window at nothing all day long, and his mom put the youngest of his brothers and sisters up for adoption, sending him into town to work at a local gas station. He tried to drop out of school to work more hours, but a truant officer came around the station and put the fear of God into the owner, who made him go back.

By now, Gideon was tall and athletic but with no funds to join any kind of a sports team, so he considered joining the military after high school. The local kids teased him about his ragged looks, so he started stealing clothes from the local Woolworths just so he would have clean pants and shirt for Friday sock hops when he could cop a feel under someone's trainer bra for free until he got tossed. But some of the girls let him do it, even let him show what he'd learned from Annabelle. He excelled at doing the Frenchie thing with his tongue in their little wet holes. Hell, they'd even line up for him.

The station owner, for his graduation present, offered to lend him his Lincoln and gave him some money so he could take a date to dinner and the prom. His date was a cute redhead going straight into beauty school after graduation. He loved the way her lashes flittered about, the way she talked incessantly but made his dick hard as he watched her little pink tongue dart around super-white teeth. Oh, what he dreamed she could do with that tongue. And he'd show her what he could do too. She liked to chew gum and wore her hair out in a big, scooped flip that looked like a ski jump. He had the urge to muss it up every time he saw her, almost as much as he had the urge to dive under her petticoats and kiss the lips of her sex and make her cry for him.

Gideon thought about that night of the prom. The Italian restaurant was decked out in twinkle lights, opera music wafting softly in the background. He ordered an eggplant dish because it was the cheapest on the menu. She, of course, had to have steak, but only ate a couple of bites, which pissed him off. The waiter brought him a doggie bag he slipped under his seat for later.

They stayed at the prom for about four or five dances, and soon it was obvious if he didn't relieve himself he'd rupture a vein in his groin. They smoked cigarettes and sipped on some cheap wine he'd stolen from his dad. The more she drank, the bigger her smile and the more she needed help standing, which was all right with him. In fact, she didn't mind when he held her with one hand and snaked his other hand up the inside of her creamy thigh. When he slipped his finger under the elastic at the top of her leg she jumped. Jumped right onto his finger.

As he twirled around in her little opening, he saw the beads of sweat form on her softly haired upper lip.

Her eyes crossed as she leaned back, showing him her long neck. The porcelain of her skin was intoxicating. She wore a little cross he bent to cover with his mouth. He slipped his tongue down between her breasts as he pushed his way under the top of her scooped-neck prom dress.

All the petticoats and fabric was annoying him, but he didn't want to take his finger out of her opening, especially seeing what it was doing to her. So he slid the top of her dress over her shoulders, first one, and then the other, and was surprised to see that the whole thing would slide right off her. He removed his fingers and watched her when he inserted them into his mouth. She laughed and then leaned in to him to have a little lick. She was hot for everything. He was of a mind to do it all, too.

All she had left was her panties, which she slid down herself.

"Hey, Gideon, not fair. I'm naked, and you still have everything on."

He didn't want to scare her with his concrete hard cock, but she asked for it. He unbuttoned the top button of his shirt and she did the rest while he unbuckled his belt and unzipped his jeans. Right as rain, his shaft bounced out, engorged and ready to play.

"Oh, my!"

Damn it. She's seen one before.

"Does every guy look like this?" she asked. Her fingers were all over him.

"That feels real good, Georgette. Squeeze it a little."

She obliged, but still had an unanswered question. "My brother doesn't look like this."

"No, only those men with special powers do."

"Special powers?"

"We're created to bring pleasure to women. And they never get pregnant. I'm like an angel. An angel of sex."

"An angel! Honest?"

Gideon didn't have a problem with this lie. He thought he would give her something, some experience she could think about for the rest of her life. It wasn't totally self-serving. But he smirked when he answered her, "Sure. Why do you think I'm named Gideon? Right out. Of. The. Bible." She had made a ring of her fingers and was sliding up and down his member, just like Annabelle had done. "You done this before, honey?"

"I saw one of my brother's picture books on sex."

"Well, you're a natural, honey... squeeze just a... little... harder... *please!*"

"So, Gideon, you're an angel, sent from God and all?"

"Yes, ma'am." He smiled down on her as she kneeled, and being a natural, she touched her tongue to the helmet of his penis. A little drop of precum remained as she took one long lick.

"Tastes funny."

"It changes flavors. You'll see."

She had him so worked up he could hardly walk, but he bent over and made a bed of their clothes, and with the pink rayon of her ruby-edged petticoats popping up between his legs, he extended his hand and pulled her down on top of him.

"See, God gave us these special powers, so we could show you how it's done. And, since we aren't really men, you are still a good girl."

"You sure?"

He looked into her bright green eyes, her peach complexion, and made a promise to God and anyone else who would listen. *If she'll let me fuck her, I'll only take redheads for the rest of my life. I'll pass up the chocolate ones, the blondes, and brunettes. I'll just limit myself to redheads. So help me God. Give me this one.*

"Angels never lie, honey. You know that."

It was the last thing he heard in his dream. Opening his eyes, he pondered his encounter with his past, the lady stuck on the bus and how confusing it all was now. They were like two ram goats charging against each other, both sides of his personality, each just as strong as the other. One was familiar and one all new, but exciting. The internal tug at his soul made his heart pound, made the bed rattle, caused the little nymph at his side to stir, while he pondered his fate. Was one side going to kill the other? Or could they both learn to live together?

Almost as if he'd foretold his own future, "I'm an angel," he'd told her way back then. And, in a twist of fate he would later discover, that Supreme Being answered his call. But he'd made a deal, and a deal was a deal. So, over the next few years as his sexual appetites developed and even after he was turned vampire, he made sure he tried to nail every redhead he met, and very nearly succeeded.

CHAPTER 7

PERSEPHONE WATCHED GIDEON and his lover resting, sweat glistening over both their bodies. She'd seen couples having sex before, but she'd not seen the healing touch nor the biting and blood beforehand. It was not something they'd trained her for up in the Guardianship. She needed to get more information, but now she was suddenly shy about asking Father about it, fearing some kind of reprisal.

He must already know this is how it's done.

But it had never come up as the topic of conversation with her Guardian friends, and surely, if someone else saw what she'd just witnessed, someone would say something about it.

She was proud of her detachment. The sexual urge was strong with them, but it wasn't for her, and that was a good thing. Some human things remained of her. Some of her memories were still there, but this, even if she'd had sex before she was turned, was not one of those memories that clung to her.

Not that she wasn't curious. His shoulders were larger than she remembered and his face more angular. He seemed to have doubled the muscles she remembered in the Guardianship. His dark angel nature had indeed had its way with his body, altering it yet again.

Poor Gideon. Her detachment was slipping, but it was hard not to feel sorrow for the person she knew had goodness inside him. Somewhere, it was buried there still.

She'd always imagined his lovemaking would be something beautiful, pure, and fulfilling, something that would be more than grunting, rutting like an animal, biting and sweating, tearing of sheets, and screaming. Surely this wasn't how the human population did things. Maybe it was the vampire way.

As she watched the girl sleeping, she became aware of a dark presence looming over the bed, spying on the sleeping couple just as she was. Whatever it was, Father's protection must have cloaked her because the shadow traveled with long spiral tendrils, curling around body parts, rubbing up against thighs and cheeks and across their lips, as if craving both of them. It was dangerous and very odd. But whatever it was, it didn't seem to sense Persephone sitting there on top of the dresser.

Being extra careful, she held her breath and remained motionless. The girl moaned and arched up, slightly elevating off the ground as if held by an unseen hand.

Gideon stirred, and the girl's body floated back down, snuggling against him. But the dark figure remained. Again the long tendrils wrapped around her body, and she was lifted and then covered, like in a shroud.

Persephone's heart was racing. Should she wake Gideon? Should she intervene? Persephone didn't know if she could even stop the dark being from taking the woman. But if it came for Gideon, well then she'd have to act. She'd been ordered to look after him, even at the cost of her own life.

She considered sending a telepathic message but wasn't sure if it would alert the evil creature now taking its prize. Just as quickly as the being appeared, it was gone, and with it, the girl.

Persephone wasn't sure if it was the right thing to do, but she made a decision. She needed to tell him about the shadow figure, but she needed to clear the air first. Perhaps now would be a good time to quickly apologize to him for the pain she'd caused him. Maybe he could take his anger out on her, or attempt to. She was fairly sure Father's protection would make it impossible for him to hurt her. And that was just something she was going to have to trust.

She stood in the middle of the floor, became visible, and ran to Gideon's side.

"Gideon, Gideon. You must waken."

He whirled around, his eyes growing wide, appearing to turn red. His lips curled up to the right in a grimace as he growled, like he'd done so many times in the Guardianship.

"You!" He flew for her, hands out as if to choke her, but just before impact, his body hit a protection field, and he was knocked to the floor, dazed. Then he attempted to repeat his lunge toward her and again was repelled. That's when she noticed he was naked. She averted her eyes, but spoke to him from the side.

"It's no use. Father's protection covers me."

Gideon wasn't paying attention. He was throwing glass bowls, a wine bottle, then a lamp. He threw a chair and even a small table, creating a fine rain of wood splinters and glass throughout the bedroom area. His feet were bleeding from his pacing over the broken material. He tried to remove tufts of his own hair from his scalp.

Persephone gently flicked some dust toward Gideon, and it made him sneeze.

"No! You, stop that. I'm immune to your little

tricks."

"You need to calm down, Gideon."

"You need to die. You're the bitch who ruined my life."

"Won't solve anything to be upset. And we don't have time."

"Upset?" he mimicked with his face making a sour prune expression. "What the hell do you know about upset?" He stopped pacing and stood tall, pointing to the ceiling. "And time? I've got all the time in the fuckin' world. You need to go home. Get out of my life and never come back."

"Gideon, please, hear me out. Let me talk to you."

"I'm done with the talking. We have nothing to say to each other. You've done enough. I don't need anything from you. I don't want anything from you or your Supreme Being."

"Gideon, I have something extremely important to tell you, but first, I want to take responsibility for the pain I've caused you. It is my fault you're going through all this."

"Damn right. You understand now what you did?"

"Yes, I do. And again, I'm very, very sorry."

"Apology not accepted."

"You shouldn't have to bear this burden all alone. Let me help you."

"You've done more than enough to fuck up my life. I'm going to make it my mission to fuck up yours if you don't stop pestering me. Now leave me alone. *Now!*"

"Hear me out, please. It's important."

"Didn't you get it the first time? You are the last person in the whole universe I want to see right now. Besides, I'm not alone!" He turned to point to the bed, where she knew he was expecting to see the girl. The girl he'd forgotten about when he saw Persephone. He hit his palm to his forehead, and staggered back several steps.

"I've been sent to help you."

"I don't need your help. I don't need the big guy's help. I guess I'm on my own now. Just waiting for the gates of Hell to welcome me. You've even scared off my... my... friend."

"But it doesn't have to be that way. That's what I'm trying to tell you."

"Says who?"

"Like I said, I've been sent to you."

"But I just told you I don't need anybody. Do you have to insert yourself into everything I do? Can't you leave me alone?" he said, standing naked in front of her. Persephone closed her eyes, balling her hands into fists. "Not looking, Gideon." She heard rustling coming from Gideon's direction.

"I'm decent."

Well, he had jeans on, but he was anything but decent. His powerful, broad shoulders and muscled chest was a thing of beauty. He was bigger than she remembered him. When he turned to slip on some old shoes, she saw the large wing sacs, much bulkier than any Guardian anatomy. His dark angel status made him look mean. She found herself staring at him and then remembered the girl. "The girl—Ashley. I've come to help you, to warn you!"

"I think you've done enough already. Spying on me, were we?" He growled. "Get any tips or pointers? I know you Guardians and your dirty little secrets. You watched, didn't you, angel?"

She had no choice but to hang her head in shame. Her cheeks were flaming.

"And for your information, I don't need your help with any of my women. Is that understood?"

She couldn't look at him. He was swearing under his breath, pacing back and forth.

"Now go away and leave me alone," he boomed. "I'm not doing the Supreme Being's dirty work any longer. So, for what it's worth, you're *fired*."

She began to cry. Trying as hard as she could, she couldn't stop herself from shaking.

"And stop crying."

That jolted her back to reality. She was used to following orders, but not so harshly spoken.

He scanned the room and then ran out into the hallway, calling Ashley's name to the rest of the huge empty house. "So where is she? Some Guardian you are."

"She's been taken, Gideon. That's what I'm trying to tell you."

"Taken? Taken by whom?"

"It was this black, smoke-like figure with long snaky arms or something." She wiggled her fingers out to the sides like tiny tentacles, holding her arms close to her body. Then she wiped her nose on the sleeve of her white gown. "I've never seen anything like it," she finally said.

"Did the thing make any sounds? Talk? Summon her or anything? Have a face?"

"No face. Just a smoke cloud."

"Shit."

Persephone put her hand to her mouth. She'd meant to put her hands to her ears but didn't react in time.

"Where did they go?"

She pointed to the wall. That made Gideon angry. He suddenly burst before her in a flash. She could hear his heavy breathing, feel the heat of his huge body standing very close, menacing her. He angled his head slowly like he had a stiff neck and gradually squinted, pointing to the wall. "There's no window or doorway there."

Persephone was shaking again. Her sniffles made it difficult to talk. "Y-Yes. I know. They went *through* the wall." She wiped her nose again.

Gideon let out a stream of invectives. Persephone was glad she didn't understand half of them. He peered out the bedroom window overlooking the vineyard valley floor, totally obstructed by the night, then opened the double doors to the upstairs deck, peering in the direction of their exit. He searched the horizon, even looking straight above him into the night stars. Nothing he saw snagged his attention.

"Why didn't you wake me?" he said when he came back in, closing the doors behind him.

"I was worried for your safety."

"I was fuckin' asleep! Can't get much more vulnerable than that. I should have defended her."

"I would have defended *you* if the creature had come after you."

"Oh God, what a comforting thought!" He bent down on one knee as if praying to underscore his sarcasm.

"My contract is not with her. It's with you. Besides, that thing didn't even see me. I don't think."

He pulled away, righting himself, standing tall in the middle of the room, still shirtless but looking so strong. Such a perfect specimen, even if he was a fallen Guardian. His black wing sacs began to gape open, and she took that to mean he intended to fly off somewhere. Then he drew in a huge breath. Letting it out, he dropped his head. His shoulders hung like a rag doll on a peg.

He brought his hands to his eyes.

"What can I do to help?" she asked.

Gideon returned a nasty glare. His nostrils flared, and even his eyes appeared to be turning red. "You can let me think!"

He started to concentrate again, and then he stopped, turning in her direction.

"No. On second thought, get out of here!" He pointed to the door then the ceiling.

"Gideon, I know I don't look like I'm very strong, but I can do things to help you. Maybe I can get some help from the Guardianship."

He was about to scream another "No" at her when they heard the downstairs door open. A male voice called out in a British accent, "Yo, Gideon, where the fuck are you, you bloody asshole?"

"Don't go anywhere," Gideon whispered. "Stay right here," he commanded. He dashed for the bedroom doorway arch, calling out downstairs, "Francis, I'm coming down right now." He grabbed a shirt and then thought better of it, tossing it to the ground, and then closed the door behind him, leaving her alone.

She tilted her head, thinking perhaps another thought would drift in that would help make her predicament more clear.

She thought about all the images of everything that had transpired today: the lonely tower with the fog rolling in, the athletic lovemaking with the girl, the dark shadow who stole her away. And then she recalled seeing him rest on the bed, trying to be quiet so the girl could sleep. Persephone at that moment felt the rumble of Gideon's heart, beating against her own, even from the space clear across the room. His heart wasn't evil. It was warm, full of the manliness she'd experienced in human males. A human hero.

He was somehow innocent, yet possessed strange, dark powers. These powers were like armaments to his body, enhancements or prosthetics protecting him. Gideon was a tenderhearted soul trapped in a warrior's body that had been altered. *Thrice* altered. And she'd been the cause of one of those, sadly.

Redemption is so complicated!

She was glad it wasn't her job to sort all this out. Way beyond her pay grade. Perhaps if Father knew all about this, he'd decide Gideon was more trouble than he was worth. Thus, if she were going to save Gideon from himself, from the evil forces out there, from the Underworld, from this dark creature, the girl or whatever else out there he was battling, perhaps she'd also have to keep this little secret from Father.

It was just a *little* secret anyway, she told herself. *Really* insignificant, compared to the importance of all humanity. Surely in the end, he wouldn't mind, as long as she got the desired result.

She heard heated voices downstairs and could not bear to be left out of any of Gideon's secrets. She tiptoed to the door, opened it, and peered over the railing.

CHAPTER 8

"Jesus, Gideon. You really fucked up." Francis's contorted face had never looked so hideous, so full of contempt. The over-six-foot angel, plagued with allergies, even to his own wings, was Gideon's only friend. Francis's next comment was truncated by a series of loud uncontrollable sneezes punctuated with howling farm-animal bellows sounding like half-ostrich honk and half-squealing mother pig. Getting control of his breath finally, he pulled a large tablecloth of a mankerchief from his back pocket and sneezed into it again, nearly doing a cartwheel in the hallway right in front of Gideon.

"Francis, get hold of yourself."

"What the bloody hell's that foul smell?"

Gideon shrugged and watched Francis lose himself in his oversized hanky again and then blow his nose hard enough to make the windows rattle.

"Goddammit, Gideon, you're eating duck again!"

"No. No ducks. No fowl of any kind." Gideon was smug, wrapping his arms around his own waist and waited for Francis to recover.

"Parakeets. Canaries. You have a bird in here somewhere."

"You forget, Francis, I am an angel, same as you. If you're allergic to your own feathers, perhaps you are also allergic to these." Gideon arched back in a near-ballet pose with his arms outstretched above him and his black wings unfurled, knocking a mirror off the wall and overturning an étagère and a huge potted African fern. Francis's eyes got wide, laced with fear and panic as his whites began turning a light shade of pink on their way to red.

"Stop it. Stop them!" Francis screamed, nearly inhaling his mankerchief and then sneezing so hard the dirty, white linen flew in Gideon's face. Francis righted himself from his involuntary bow and whipped the cloth away. "I am *NOT* contagious!"

Gideon gave him a lopsided half smile. He could see Francis's own wings had become unraveled, bulging out his upper collar like a hunchback. A few dirty white feathers settled on the expensive Persian foyer runner at their feet—the only telltale sign Francis was indeed an angel at all. Normally his wings drooped limply, scraping the ground as he walked, following like a couple of errant children. His black trench coat had come untied and was hanging off one shoulder. His white shirt was sticking to his skinny, pink upper torso. Because Francis refused to wear an undershirt, Gideon could see his nipples and his palm-print-sized patch of dark chest hair. The angel's belt had come unbuckled and his fly was nearly halfway unzipped. Gideon chose that feature to point to next, and Francis fixed himself, grumbling.

"This is your doing," he said. "I am not sick."

"No. Just flawed. So get it over with, Francis. Say what you came to say and then let's move on, shall we?"

Francis's chest heaved as he paced back and forth on the burgundy rug in Gideon's foyer. His eyes darted about, his hands whipped at his sides, searching for something to grasp, something to do.

Something to hit.

"I know you're angry, Francis," Gideon began.

"Put those goddamned wings away, Gideon, so we can talk. My God, those are twice the size of your old ones. You reek of bird hormones."

The simple adjustment in Gideon's over-developed trapezius muscles packed his wings back into their skin sacs. He was proud of his own control, all done without a single dark feather falling out of line. Francis had not been paying a bit of attention.

The older angel smelled from the exertion of tracing against the wind of the storm now blowing. He didn't like to fly but not using his wings made the work much more strenuous. He also had been drinking red wine, and it stained the area above his upper lip on the left side. His blondish-gray hair stood out in all directions in stiff tufts from not being combed in days. For the first time, Gideon detected light stubble on Francis's chin. It was slightly red.

You old Viking, you.

Francis searched the foyer and then poked his head into the kitchen. He shrugged. "So what happened?" His hands were waist high, palms up. Then he fell on his knees, grabbing his nose rag just in time to stop another sneeze.

"I couldn't do it anymore, Francis," Gideon said to the top of the angel's head.

Francis swore and then got on his feet again, sighing. He rolled his neck. "What, you just decided yesterday you were going to ruin your own life and the lives of all the other angels and humans out there? Whatever were you thinking, Gideon? You've caused a huge stir. I haven't seen so many Guardians for years, all crying and wailing about, wondering where you went and why."

"And what have you told them?"

Francis scrunched up his face. "Told them? What *could* I tell them? I had no fuckin' clue. You just go nuts or something? Is this a vampire-hormone-male-menopause kind of thing here?" he said from behind his mankerchief.

"No, it's not like that at all. I just—" Gideon shook his head. "You know how we are. Controlled. Everything is regimented."

"We got free will."

"Ya think?"

"Well, within reason. As long as we get the job done."

"I have to sit up there on that fuckin' tower six days a week, asshole. You only have to do it one."

"That's because I tend a flock. I do social work. You know that." Francis swung his cloth around like he was hailing a waiter.

"And why can't I walk around the streets of San Francisco, sit in coffee houses, and talk to girls like you do?"

"You know why."

"*Enlighten* me."

"Because I'm not gonna do anything. I think the man upstairs was always worried about you. After all I saw today, could you blame him?"

Gideon could feel Francis had calmed down, but only slightly.

"So you went on a bender," his friend began, "and I love you like a brother, Gideon, but I'm not taking your fuckin' job. You take a little time off. Get yourself right in the head, and then you come back. All is forgiven."

"I don't think so."

"Well, it better be fuckin' so because I ain't—" He sneezed again. "—doin' that job for you. He's gonna have to get someone else."

"See, *you* don't even want that job," Gideon jabbed.

"Don't start with me. *Nobody* wants that job. But there has never been anyone like you, either."

"Francis, you're forgetting something important. Suppose he's gonna scorch me? A Fallen Angel can't be a Watcher. You know that. Hell, I don't even know what the hell is going to happen to me. I didn't really plan all this out. You really think the Guardianship would be okay with a Dark doing that position? No, someone else's got to do it. That someone won't be me. I got enough of my own problems."

Francis hesitated, pondering what Gideon had just told him. "I'll tell you what. You're gonna have to get some protection. One thing when you were a new Guardian and all that, you kinda had the best of both worlds. Your vampire nature, some of it remained, right?"

"Right."

"And then you had protection from Him. But now? I mean, you know that little one-legged Russian angel who went dark? It was fun for a time, but man, he didn't look very good last time he visited. Remember?"

"Yeah, I kicked him off the bridge."

"He brought you that red vodka and thought he was going to get you so drunk you'd let him escort you down there. You refused."

"I wasn't ready. Look, Francis, I don't want to go to the Underworld. I just want to stay here, in the human world. Where I can think and—"

"Chase the ladies, I know. I could never understand His problem with that." Francis trusted himself enough to refold and stow his towel into his back pocket.

"Agreed, Francis." He glanced upstairs and saw Persephone in the shadows at the landing. That made Francis take notice.

"Aha! So I interrupted you. Why didn't I think of that?" Francis stepped under the light in the middle of the foyer and raised one arm, wiggling his fingers. "Come on out here, sweetheart. Let's see what the cat dragged in."

Gideon grabbed Francis around his neck and tried

to put a chokehold on him. His friend slipped out of his grasp and disappeared to another corner.

"I don't fuckin' fly, but I haven't lost the gift of tracing. Don't you try anything on me."

"Gideon, it's okay." Persephone's voice was steady. She stepped to the edge of the landing and placed her little pink hands on the metal railing. She was the true picture of a perfect Guardian angel. Her long blonde hair cascaded around her flawless pale skin. The picture of innocence and grace. Unblemished perfection. In spite of himself, he felt his heart skip a couple beats. It was the first time he'd gazed upon a woman other than a redhead and thought she was stunningly beautiful.

Francis gasped and Gideon gave him a warning growl.

But Gideon also noticed something else. She did not wear panties. What he could see under her delicate white gown made him blush. He got the impression she didn't know any better. He was entranced until he realized Francis had also taken a good look.

"*Hallo,* little Miss Guardian. Holy crap, Gideon, you are sure playing with fire."

Gideon swore under his breath.

"I was sent," Persephone said in her melodic voice, as she made her way down the stairs. Her bare feet made not a sound. A hushed pall fell between the two angel friends.

Francis suddenly traced next to Gideon and whispered, "You gotta get some clothes on that angel, especially—"

"Shoes," Gideon interrupted. "But she's not staying long," he finished. He tried to give her a glare or show his displeasure with her near-nakedness but found he was unable to. Her sweet pink face disarmed him again.

"That's not for you to decide, Gideon," Persephone said as she addressed Francis. "I'm Persephone, Gideon's Guardian. And you are Francis, is that right?"

Francis walked up to the young angel, and, with a slight downward angle of his head and shoulders, bowed, taking her hand, and kissing her knuckles. "Francis, friend to Gideon, part-time Watcher, and Guardian as yourself. Completely at your service, Persephone." Gideon watched Francis inhale her scent without covering up his arousal. He let go of her hand quickly, grabbing his towel and stopping another sneeze. Persephone's arm floated gently down next to her side like a snowflake.

Gideon watched his angel friend peruse Persephone's body and saw the resulting blush on her face. He growled in a slow rumble only Francis would be able to hear.

"Charming. I can see why you're so smitten," Francis whispered.

"Touch one hair on her head and I'll end you."

"It's not like that. I'm his *Guardian*," interrupted Persephone.

"*My* Guardian was an old hag. It was not a pleasant experience." Francis again folded his towel. Gideon found himself growling again to ward off his friend's interest.

She turned and defiantly focused on Gideon. "I think the three of us need to have a little chat."

"Bloody hell." Francis put his hands on his hips and shrugged. "We do need some answers and fast. I'd kinda like to hear what she has to say," he said to Gideon.

"You don't know the whole story," Gideon answered.

"Well, maybe he can help, Gideon. We've got to tell him." She wasn't going to be deterred.

"Now what? Tell him what, exactly?" asked Francis, following Gideon and Persephone into the living room. Gideon turned on the gas fireplace but no lights. Four tall-backed, red, leather chairs were positioned in front of the stone hearth, two facing two. He motioned for his guests to have a seat.

Persephone tucked her legs under her and curled up on one of the seats closest to the fireplace. Gideon tried not to look, but again failed. It was everything he could do not to stare at his Guardian's beauty, something he'd never allowed himself to consider when he was in training. It was like he was seeing her for the first time.

"Come on. Out with it," insisted Francis after he sat down across from them, his elbows on his knees. "Next you'll say you two are expecting, or she's one of their bots or some dumb shit like that."

No one moved so Francis continued with another guess. "You got married?"

"No!" Both Persephone and Gideon shouted him back.

"Oh, this must be really delicious." Francis turned to Persephone. "*You're* not supposed to lie. I'm counting on this." His finger waggled accusingly.

"I met someone special on the bus," Gideon blurted-ed, taking the heat off his Guardian.

Francis sat back in the chair, crossed his arms and legs, and placed a hand over his forehead. "Oh God, this sounds like a boring story already."

"He drove a bus off the Golden Gate Bridge, Francis. But he rescued her."

"Yes, I was going to ask you how you managed to

do that."

"My Carl Gustav did a great job." Gideon grinned. "My wings and sexual prowess did the rest."

They heard pounding on the roof, and Francis scurried to his feet. "Oh God, you've brought them."

"No, Francis, it's a branch. I've got to have it trimmed."

"Brought whom?" asked Persephone.

"The inky ones. Disgusting creatures," said Francis as he shuddered. "You sure about that sound? Because you're a magnet for dark things now, and we aren't trained, well, you know," mumbled Francis.

"Stop it, Francis. Yes. I recognize the sound." Gideon lifted a white feather off his thigh and dropped it on the carpet.

"Before sunrise, we need to make a plan, Gideon." Persephone was all business. She addressed Francis next. "Gideon was asleep in bed with *her* when some dark, shadowy figure stole the girl away, just carried her out into the night."

Francis looked to Gideon, who nodded.

"You ever see anything like that?" she asked.

Gideon had been musing on what his Guardian had seen of the sexual encounter with Ashley and hoped she'd arrived after they were asleep.

"Our old friend Luther talked about those Dark

Ones. Yuck." Francis shuddered again. "You'll be pulled below, and it won't be pretty."

"How do you know this?" Gideon faced his friend.

"Luther saw it. He had a friend who was dragged out of bed. He wanted to save his woman from the creature."

"And did he?"

"The thing that got him laughed in his face and urinated on her."

Gideon hadn't considered anything dangerous would happen to Ashley. But now he realized it was possible. "What did the thing look like?"

"Big, black, skinny angel with shiny bat-like wings and long yellow fangs. Luther ran into the room just as the thing pulled out his huge pecker and sprayed the girl. Disgusting! He held the guy by the neck, and try as he might, his arms were too short to be able to deliver blows to the beast. All he could do was scream and try to bite."

Gideon was silent.

"The ugly angel of death flew through the window with both of them, screaming for help that would never come. The guy, stark naked, flailed in its claws. And it was laughing at them both."

"Has Luther seen them since?"

"Nope. No one has seen any of them, at least none

of our crowd anyways."

Gideon considered this new information. He'd thought there would be some sort of welcoming committee, some official sign that he was now among the fallen and would be claimed in some ceremony, like a coronation. He was not just an ordinary angel, after all. He was a Watcher, next best thing to a full-blooded Guardian, who was prized highest in the ranks of the Fallen. He thought maybe he could meet the leadership, negotiate some things, and then he would find Ashley, once everything was arranged to his liking. This story about abductions and Ashley being taken wasn't at all what Gideon had in mind.

"So who runs the place? Who do they report to? Where do they take them?" Gideon hadn't completely believed Persephone's tale about the abduction, but with Francis's confirmation, he now understood what danger Ashley was in. It also meant Persephone was also in more danger than he could protect her from.

"We have no clue. We're Guardians, and we never got training in this," said Francis. Persephone was agreeing. Gideon didn't like the fact that Francis had aligned himself with her, and now it was two against one.

"So who can help us? I mean, surely someone knows," she asked.

Francis stood, gazing into the fire as if the answers to all their questions resided there. "I think we need to go visit the clockmaker."

CHAPTER 9

PERSEPHONE HAD NEVER ridden in a large vehicle before. Though the ceiling height was tall she still felt hemmed in, but it was the best they could do. Gideon couldn't trace with both of them. Francis refused to fly and Persephone had never transported except to bring her charges to Heaven. So they drove.

Gideon's driving was erratic. He and Francis were bantering back and forth from the front seat while Persephone examined her perch on the bench seat behind. Looking over her shoulder, she noticed the black canvas bag filled with tools and other assorted things, perhaps weapons Gideon liked to take with him. So the rumors were true.

"So who is this guy anyway, Francis?"

"We call him the clockmaker."

"That doesn't tell me shit. I'm not in the market for a clock."

"You are because you're out of time," quipped

Francis.

"He makes time or clocks?"

"I honestly don't know what or how he does anything. I just know that he knows a whole lot about the Underworld and the way things work. He takes things apart to study how they're made. He makes things."

"What things?"

"Things that move. Things that fly. Things that do other things." Francis's voice trailed off as he watched rain hit the passenger window.

"He know we're coming?"

"Fuck no. I don't even know if he'll see you. I'm hoping she can get us in." Francis tilted his head to her direction.

"Francis, do I know this man?" Persephone was racking her brain to try to come up with some past reference, but the *Clockmaker* tag wasn't helping.

"I don't think so. And he's not a man."

"What is he then?" Her blood pressure was beginning to spike. It was exciting to be on a mission, and a dangerous one at that. But although her excitement was thrilling, she feared she might not be able to protect her charge.

"Couldn't say." Francis looked straight ahead, and she could tell he was done talking. He pointed to the right, and Gideon's tires squealed over the wet pavement. Street lamps were getting fewer and fewer as they wound their way back and forth through alleyways. She'd have to use her automatic homing device to get anywhere familiar. All the buildings began to look the same. The neighborhood was made up of small shops with several stories above. Nearly every window was dark.

"Are we close?" Gideon asked as he squeezed the steering wheel, making the black leather covering groan as if it were alive.

"Very. So slow down and I need to concentrate to find it. Just a little shop."

"A clock shop."

"You'll see."

Gideon abruptly pulled over. "Dammit, Francis. I got to have answers, and I got to have them now. I can't just walk into any place with her. You know that. I have no idea who this guy is or even if he's a good guy or a bad buy."

Francis cackled, and it gave Persephone shudders.

"That's the thing. I have no clue. But I do know he has some answers. And that's what we need most. You may not like to hear them, but he'll have them, if anyone does. And then you can decide your next course of action. Without some of this information, I think you'd better prepare yourself to become a scorched oily patch on the floor somewhere."

"Jeez. Not a very nice picture," Gideon said as he pulled out slowly into the deserted street. He examined his rearview mirror and caught Persephone's eye. "You scared yet, kid?"

She checked herself. She wasn't scared for herself. She had been afraid for Gideon, but that had vanished as she anticipated a meeting with some strange being with questionable motives.

"I will protect you, Gideon."

"Dammit, Persephone. Stop saying that. You have no clue what that even means." Gideon's tone rubbed her already raw emotions. It was what they called *heart bleeding*, the harsh knowledge her efforts were not being appreciated but she had to go on anyway.

"Doesn't matter. I'm not throwing in the towel. I'm here to do my job."

Her charge was going to say something else unkind, but Francis grasped his forearm. "Gideon, lighten up on her. At least one of us knows what their job is. Leave it be for now. This won't do you any good."

Gideon made a quick glance in the mirror again, and their eyes met. "Sorry."

It was the first apology she'd heard from him. Some evidence that the soul inside his strange circumstance had the capacity for compassion. It was a very good sign.

"Stop right here and pull over," Francis commanded. "He's right here."

She saw the tiny shop, dimly lit from within, cluttered with moving parts and faces of timepieces like watching fish in an aquarium. Small animals and carved figurines of clowns, kings, moons, and stars moved along little tracks, everything in motion, casting various shapes and shadows against the walls and the sidewalk in front of the shop. The painted, antique-looking letters in the window read *"Clockworks Unlimited."*

A second sign hanging from the shop door that read *Out Of Time.*

"This guy have a sense of humor?" Gideon frowned at his Guardian friend.

"I doubt it. He's not that way."

"So what's with the *'Out Of Time'* sign?"

"I've never thought about that. I'll ask him." Francis opened his door. "I think I'll approach with your Guardian, while you wait in the truck, if you don't mind."

"As if I have a choice."

"Your funeral. We have to handle this guy with kid gloves." Frances squinted and then peered up to the windows above the shop. "He's kinda weird. Hard to think what goes on in that mind of his. I'm guessing he has a lot of moving parts that look something like this." Francis pointed to a flock of mechanical birds flying inside the window in loose formation.

"Are those real?" Persephone noticed a cloud of small buzzing insects hovering over the archway of the front door on the outside of the building.

"Yup. Real bots." Francis grinned at Gideon, rain soaking his right shoulder and running down his front. "They're as real as the real ones, just made up of different material, that's all. The guy's a genius."

Persephone slid out of the car. The light misting rain was a welcome relief and cooled her anxiety. Francis's parting words to Gideon were, "You stay here and we'll send a message. You still get those, don't you?"

Persephone heard Gideon call Francis an asshole.

Francis put his arm around her, and she noticed part of his left wing protruded above his collar again.

"I imagine this place has lots of dusty corners, Francis. Are your allergies going to be okay?"

"Kid, I'm not allergic to dust. Mostly feathers. These birds don't shed anything but springs, tiny screws, and pieces of cellophane. The deadly toxins in some of them are safely guarded in glass tubes under pressure. I just keep out of their way."

He knocked on the front door, and then bent to whisper to her, "And you see something crawling on the ground, best not to step on it. They are bugs all right, but not the harmless kind our Father makes."

He knocked again with more force. The cloud of insects buzzed louder and closer to the tops of their heads, which sent her into Francis's arms.

"No worries, kid. He has to have a reason to come after us. Let's not give him one." He winked and pinched her nose.

Though he was still inside his truck, she could hear Gideon growling. She took it again as a good sign that he at least cared about her welfare.

A light fixture illuminated the front door as the cloud of insects dissipated into thin air. A short round-backed man in blue overalls pressed his nose against the glass to get a better view of his company. His thick glasses made his eyes look two inches wide. He blinked and then scowled.

"Dammit, Francis. You got trouble with a new toy? Go away. It's too late." The small gentlemen behind the door looked Persephone up and down. "Uh oh. What the hell are you tampering with, Francis?"

"Let me in," Francis whispered. "I'll explain it all inside."

"Is it safe?" the man asked Persephone. She had no

idea what he meant.

"What?" she asked back.

"Is it safe?" he repeated.

Francis swore under his breath and then put his lips to her ear, even though she would be able to follow a telepathic message from him. "He knows you're a Guardian. Tell him it's okay."

"It's safe," she repeated. "And we have Gideon here in the truck, too. Can he come?"

The man's skin turned a pale shade of green in the dim light. As he shook his head, Persephone saw he had a number of small warts in clusters on his chin and sides of his cheeks. She also saw fresh sutures covered in bandages in three places along his forehead. It appeared to her the man was quite clumsy.

"Suppose it won't make any difference now. I have words for Gideon."

Persephone nodded to Gideon in the front seat as the man unlocked and opened the door. The deafening sound of clocks ticking and chiming echoed off the watery streets and walls of the alleyway.

"You could have walked right in without waking me up to do this," he said.

"That wouldn't be respectful," answered Francis.

"Right. One of your Guardian things." He motioned for them to enter while he waited for Gideon at the doorway. He placed his palm on Gideon's chest, holding him from passing. "What the hell happened to you? Or should I even bother to ask?"

The cloud of bugs returned, hovering menacing above Gideon's scalp.

"Contrary to what you might have heard, I'm harmless," Gideon said boldly.

The man allowed her charge to enter, adding, "And clueless. I serve tea and no alcohol." The door slammed behind him. His feet slid across the floor in brown knit slippers. As he passed her, Persephone smelled clove and cinnamon, plus some other spices she could not place. He carefully negotiated three wooden steps, making use of the creaky handrail, and continued toward an open door to a well-lit room beyond. Francis followed him while Gideon waited in the rear.

The shop was full of moving timepieces of all sizes. Pieces of metal from kitchen utensils, pots and pans, gardening tools, and even small motors were blended with clock faces, hands made of various materials, each piece inching up or down or around in circles, causing a chain reaction of other moving parts like an antique conveyor belt powered by some inscrutable source. She noticed the mechanical devices measured and told time in a variety of ways, but nothing appeared to be causing the movements except weights and momentum from other moving parts. There didn't appear to be any electricity or gas present. The only light appeared to be from flickering candles.

The blue and green flock of tiny mechanical birds flew overhead again, several of them swerving to avoid hitting her head, but not managing to avoid hitting the spoke of a slowly rotating large wheel the size of a man's head. Three of the little creatures dropped to the floor and buzzed in circles before taking flight again to join the rest of the flock. Gideon's arm about her waist helped her gently step up to follow Francis. She found the warmth of his hand lingering on the small of her back comforting, but she desperately wanted to investigate the curious devices nearly obstructing their path.

Warm breath at her ear spoke volumes. "Later. Let's go inside where it is safer."

That's exactly how she felt as Gideon went out of his way to protect her from low-hanging limbs of dolls, airplane propellers, and hanging metal baskets of spare parts. There wasn't one moving thing that resembled anything she'd ever seen before.

The large room off the shop was the gentleman's real inner sanctum with bookshelves filled with old tomes, wooden boxes with more parts overflowing from their tops, and benches with half-finished projects held together with clamps and screws. But for the lack of elves, this might have been Santa's workshop to a child, Persephone thought, similar to pictures she'd seen in Christmas books for the young. Faces of dolls with eyes that opened and closed like marionettes, working in tandem with gaping mouths shaped like the orifices of nutcrackers, formed a moving valance along one wall. The clicking of moving parts, ticking time-pieces, and occasional pings, bongs, and tympanic tapping of alarms wiped out any noise from the group's movements or the background noise of a vintage movie being wound by a mechanical hand.

The clockmaker moved several drones from a painted red table, located three additional chairs and motioned for the group to sit while he padded off to a wood-burning stove with a large silver kettle steaming in the corner. Four mismatched mugs were filled with hot water, each with its own tea bag, and placed in front of the maker's company. He removed his glasses, peeling the wire arms from around his oversized ears, putting them next to the mug and sat, waiting for someone to speak.

Persephone was uncomfortable with the silence. "Thank you for the tea."

The inventor allowed his left eyebrow to rise, a twinkle showing in his left eye, and without smiling, said, "Wait until you drink it."

Francis immediately sniffed it, raising his head to declare, "I've had it before. Actually quite delicious."

To this, the clockmaker grunted.

She and Gideon drank from their cups, the warmth on her palms soothing her nerves further. They drank quietly and in tandem.

"I know Francis. I've heard of you," he said, pointing to Gideon. "Who the hell are you, then? A Guardian, no doubt, but whatever do you want with me?"

He reached behind his back and couldn't find the spot he was looking for, then grabbed a long metal file and slid it under his collar at the rear of his neck, scratching something that itched on his upper back. His eyes closed in deep repose and pleasure, and for just a second as he reopened them, the glow was distinctly red. Persephone's system went on alert status.

"Manfred, this is Persephone, Gideon's Guardian. Persephone, Manfred the clockmaker."

His gnarled and bony hand extended over the red table, shaking. Persephone accepted the handshake tentatively. "Nice to meet you, Manfred."

"Likewise." His squeeze at the end lingered, and Persephone allowed him to withdraw first, though she was seriously creeped out by the touch. He leaned back, folding his arms across his chest, then changed his mind and inserted the file, scratching his back again.

"You want me to help you with that?" offered Francis.

"No. Keep your hands to yourself. I only touch Guardians or part-time Watchers if I initiate the contact. Not the other way around. You try to touch me," he stared at the three of them intensely one by one, "I'll rip your arm off at the shoulder socket, understood?"

Persephone felt Gideon's forearm lay beside hers on the table. Again, his touch was comforting. She could feel his impatience. She wasn't sure if Manfred could read their minds so didn't attempt to alert Francis to her question of protocol. She hoped someone would do something.

The sound of something falling in the front room startled her. Manfred was on his feet, leaning through the doorway. He discovered what he was looking for.

"Tabitha, come here and join us by the fireplace."

Persephone and the other two angels looked downward, following Manfred's lead, and all of them watched a mechanical cat waddle across the floor, its tail weaving back and forth with minute clicking sounds. The cat's eyes were also red, but luminous, as if on fire from within his skull.

"Watch it, Guardians. Tabby has a taste for real flesh and feathers, unlike myself. She likes to test my reflexes, but I assure you I never lose."

Persephone watched the "cat" rub against Manfred's fingers, sneaking a red one-eyed perusal of the company as if calculating whom to attack first.

Francis sneezed, barely getting his nose cloth out in time, which sent Tabby streaking off to a dark corner with a mechanical hiss.

"Honestly, Francis. You can do something about that, you know. That's completely disgusting. You're more like one of us. Are you entirely sure of your pedigree?"

Francis hung his head, closed his eyes, and nodded.

"Well, I'm going to begin, Manfred," Gideon started, changing the awkward subject. "We've run across a situation, and we're hoping we can get some advice from you."

"Is it serious?" the clockmaker asked.

"Deadly."

"And you trust I'll give you an honest answer? I'm not a Guardian, as you all know. And I haven't quite rid myself of the urge to trap and skin Guardians."

Persephone tensed, which drew Manfred's attention, and he followed up with a smile. "Lovely reflexes, my dear," he said as he patted her forearm. She withdrew her hand to her lap, not sure what manner of creature he was. She was fairly sure he wasn't human, mainly due to his red eyes.

"We frankly have no choice." Gideon scanned his fingers splayed on the table. "I've recently undergone a change." His upward glance to Manfred brought him face to face with an extremely nasty sneer.

"Yes. That fascinates me as well. Glad you are beginning to understand. You will be joining the Underworld soon, then?"

"I'm considering my options."

Manfred arched back, erupting in laughter. "It amazes me how He lets you remain so fuckin' naïve. After all this time, you honestly believe the whole universe subscribes to the concept of free will?"

The three angels were silent. It had never occurred to Persephone that free will wasn't a universal law of nature: Heaven, Earth, and the Underworld.

"Gideon, you *have* no options. Didn't He tell you that? You belong to the Dark One and his minions, and it is *his* will you will obey."

"You mean it's entirely about survival?" asked Francis.

"Yes! Live or be eliminated. Get them first before they end you. Survival of the fittest. Pure nature, not fuckin' nurture, that other disgusting "*N*" word. He with the biggest army wins. You don't fight unless you have to. You send someone else to their death. You don't risk anything unless you know what the outcome is in advance." He searched the faces of the three angels. "Don't they teach you anything up there? How the hell are you supposed to navigate all the big important issues? These are the things that try humans and prey on them until they have to give up. Your *father*, as you call him, has a huge hole in his fabric of perfection. A flaw the size of Montana."

"But, with all due respect, Manfred, we Guardians don't give up."

The clockmaker grinned again, overjoyed with Gideon's comment. "My dear sweet fallen angel, that's *exactly* what you did. You surrendered your perfect life for a life of chaos. Your free will snagged you in a trap you can never escape. Quite frankly, Gideon, you're fucked!"

CHAPTER 10

G IDEON WANTED TO strangle the clockmaker. He'd
been humiliated in front of his best friend and
his Guardian. And he also knew Persephone would
take it as a challenge to save him, which was *not*
something he was the least bit interested in.

He could see Francis was nervous as hell and ready
to bolt at any time.

This was buck up time, perhaps a test, and then
things might get smoother later on. Perhaps this was
his rite of passage. He'd made his statement, putting
the finger into the eye of the Supreme Being himself,
and the old guy let him do it, too. Now he had to prove
he was strong enough to survive the rules of the
Underworld. Rules were meant to be broken. Manfred
said it was chaos. Who were they to dictate what he
was to do and not do, anyway?

As he mused on it, *chaos* wasn't coming up so bad.
He'd shed his straitjacket of predictability and that

vanilla world of civil behavior, the regimented and orderly life he detested. If this was the price he would pay, so be it! He was filled with courage until he looked at the expression on Persephone's face. She was crying.

And then it hit him. While she was worried about him, he was actually worried for her own safety. Well, he'd wanted to be rid of her, but not in a cruel or rude manner. Just let her off the hook to go focus on some other soul. No reason to take up all her valuable time. Besides, he'd be sending her away for her own good.

Except he knew she was stubborn, and if anybody couldn't quit, it was Persephone. He'd have to trick her. Do something that would disgust her so badly she'd be forced to leave him as a lost cause.

And then he could concentrate on the real prize: Freedom in the belly of the Underworld. Or, free to roam in both worlds. Just not in Heaven. So, he mustn't cave in to fear. Time to *pull his pants on one leg at a time*, a throwback expression from his human days. Cinch up that belt and be a man. But in order to freely move, he had to be rid of her.

She was still shaking by his side.

"Come on, kid. He's just trying to scare you," Gideon started to explain.

Manfred had gone in search of some information, perhaps an old brochure about the place, something to prepare him more thoroughly. He imagined Ashley was awaiting his arrival with open arms, probably scared to death by that midnight flight with the black demon. If she was screaming when she was removed from his bed, he would have awakened. So all he had to do was find her and reassure her he was okay and they could spend eternity together, playing the dark side of the field.

Francis showed no expression at all, but he was beginning to sneeze more. Probably from the sweat and oils of his own white wings, as well as a little perspiration coming from Gideon.

"Maybe we should leave, Gideon. I'm not sure I need to be here for all of this."

"Chicken."

"No, man. Smart. I'm smart, Gideon. You heard what he said. Don't fight unless you already know the outcome. How can you honestly say you know the outcome of this sad story? You don't. And no amount of bravado will make me think otherwise." Francis was trying to keep emotion out of the picture, but Gideon knew he was plain scared.

"I think Francis is right. We know more now than we did before. Either way, we have to be prepared."

At last Gideon was finally getting what he wanted: to be left alone.

"Fine, then. You guys leave. I'm going to stay and figure out a few things first, and then I'll catch up with you later, or I won't. Either way, it will be my own choosing."

"I *can't* leave you here alone, Gideon." Persephone's jaw was squared, but she didn't look like any match for the clockmaker. And he was probably the lesser of the evils they'd encounter.

"This isn't your fight, angel. Now that you got a good look at things, no one will blame you for the decision to pull out, protect yourself for all the future saves you're going to make. I don't want to risk your brilliant future, rescuing souls and pleasing old SB. It's what's in your nature, Persephone. I think it's what you were *made* for."

"Sonofabitch?" Francis interrupted. "Gideon, you get away with calling Him that? Wow." Francis was shrinking more by the minute. "But hey, I think you're right. I'll just escort Persephone back, and you can check in later when you have some good news."

"No." The stubborn little Guardian was so completely pigheaded she was beginning to make him nervous.

"Angel." He took her hand and allowed her blush to make his ears buzz like static interference, despite the incessant ticking, clicking, and gongs. She was nearly melting under his gaze. He liked that she showed this reaction. Actually, it kind of excited him, if he were entirely honest. He squeezed her hand, and he experienced the exquisite smell of her wet feathers.

It even made Francis sit up and take notice.

"Honey, no hard feelings, but I'm a lost cause. You heard the man. I exercised my free will, and old SB let me do it. I made my bed, and now I'm going to lie in it. No reason to get you guys entangled. No reason at all. I got this!"

"He's got a point," his dickless angel friend tried to enlighten them.

"No. No means no. I promised. A promise is a promise."

Now Gideon was getting angry. She had once again insisted on inserting herself into his life without his permission. "Can't I just go to Hell, on my own, so we can all call it a good day?"

"That's crazy talk, and you know it." Her upper lip was quivering. Gideon was focused on it, the soft little hairs just beneath her nose, and the beads of perspiration he could smell. He wanted to lick her face, taste the sweat dribbling in unmentionable places. He couldn't take his eyes off her, even aware Francis was shaking his head from side to side, and peeking over his shoulder for signs the clockmaker was returning.

Francis knew how dangerous it was for her. Gideon was counting on his help.

"Francis? You gotta help me out here."

"I know it. Persephone, Gideon's right. We need to leave. Now."

"Oh, but we're just getting started, friends." Manfred brought a tray of fresh fruits and some exotic breads, plus a pitcher of something cold.

Ice cold.

And red.

Gideon was still holding her hand. Manfred slapped them loose. "Stop it, Gideon. You're even making *me* nervous."

The change in attitude was stark. All three angels faced the clockmaker and waited for his next comment. Depending on what the man said, it could be Gideon's cut-and-run scenario, but he stifled the thought so no telepathy could occur. He thought of dead sand crabs crusted over in seaweed. Old mattresses stuffed with musty feathers. Anything that would produce a strong image in his head to keep his plans from being discovered.

"Look. No reason to do anything tonight. I think I overwhelmed you with all these details. I apologize. I made a mistake." Manfred had his palm over his heart, but Gideon didn't believe a word of it. The wily old genius was playing with him. Playing with all of them.

"What are you proposing?" Gideon finally asked.

"We sit and drink some creature comforts from below. My dear, I would totally understand if you abstained, but you must have some fresh fruit. Just a sample of the delicacies we get to have down there. You enjoy yourself tonight, see how it all fits on you, and if you still feel uncomfortable tomorrow, we part friends."

Francis was looking to Gideon for guidance.

Gideon looked to Persephone.

"Up to you," she mumbled.

Had she decided to stop fighting? He could tell, though her answer was weak, the thought behind it was huge.

"There, see? Wasn't that easy?" Manfred presented a ruby red crystal dish filled with fresh papaya, cherries, perfectly ripe apricots, slices of orange, and several purple and yellow fruits Gideon had never seen before.

"What are these?" Francis asked as he picked up a purple-looking pear.

"I'm not going to bore you, except to say they have a strong aphrodisiac component to them. And the Red-X, well, you guys all know about Red-X, don't you? It's our finest drink and most popular item, especially with the new recruits. We're allowed unlimited quantities.

"It's habit-forming," Persephone warned.

"Really?" Manfred frowned. "Oh, I don't think so. I feed it to Tabby every day, pour it over her little kibbles."

Gideon was forcing himself not to think about the sight of this.

"Tabby's not real, Manfred." Francis had thought he was being helpful and had picked up a small tumbler of the red liqueur. He tossed it back before he could encounter the frowns from his two friends.

"Like everything these days. Moderation. A little here and there won't hurt a fly." Manfred covered his mouth after drinking his tumbler. "Or a bot fly."

"Speaking of bots, what's the purpose of all these?" asked Francis.

"These are experiments. Prototypes. You should see the big workshop we have down there. Very state-of-the-art. Everything anyone would need. Our pleasure bots aren't rough like these. We're so good at it that no one up here can tell the difference."

"So are the smoky, black things bots, too?" asked Persephone.

"Oh, you've seen one of those? That's very rare. Especially for a Guardian. But they definitely are not bots. At least not *my* bots."

"It took the girl Gideon was sleeping with," Persephone answered evenly, avoiding Gideon's sudden attention and left eye twitch.

"That's what they do," answered the clockmaker. "They retrieve the model and bring them back to be deprogrammed. They don't interfere unless someone tries to stop them. Then they can get very nasty."

Francis's far-fetched story was becoming more and more real.

"Model? As in Ashley was a model... of what... a pleasure bot?" Persephone asked the one question Gideon didn't have the courage to ask.

"Was she, Gideon?" Manfred sampled some papaya and poured himself another glass of the Red-X. The clockmaker was examining his fruit without making eye contact. "He'd know better than anyone."

Gideon's mood was darkening. He picked up his drink and drank the syrupy liquid, which went down like the cough medicine he recalled from his human days. The fire in his belly came to life, scrambling his insides, and then traveling lower into his groin region. He knew it had been unwise to partake, but he'd ignored his own admonitions. He cleared his throat and gave Manfred a straight answer.

"From what I experienced, she was perfect. The best sexual liaison I've ever had." He immediately regretted his decision to be truthful.

A ripple of something went through Persephone—a bolt of electric current as if she'd stuck her finger in a socket. Her little pink hand shakily gripped the barrel glass, and before he could stop her, she downed the whole blasted thing. Her eyes closed. Her tongue licked the excess red from her plump lips, which she sloppily smacked. It drove him crazy.

She slowly adjusted her pretty head on her long slender neck, brushing her blonde hair from her eyes with the back of her right hand, leaving it mussed up, a silly grin creeping across the angel's face.

Ashley's memory faded from his thoughts as Persephone turned her innocent beauty on him, scanning his face. Her eyes drifted down to his lips and then slowly traveled back up to meet him at the window of his soul. He saw her need and hunger for something the angel couldn't possibly understand. And she didn't try to keep him from seeing it as if her own soul stood naked before him. The spun gold of her hair contrasted with her delicate complexion, beginning to infuse into a serious blush.

At that moment, Gideon knew he was the only one in the universe who could satisfy this need. His Guardian was tethered to him with delicate golden threads so dangerous yet so compelling he had no choice at all but to welcome the entanglement. He had not only surrendered to the devils in the Underworld, he had surren-dered to his Guardian as well.

And in her eyes, he saw her willingly give herself back to him, begging to be savored.

All he had to do was find a way to take her.

CHAPTER 11

THE CLOCKMAKER HAD shaken Persephone's confidence. She wished she'd had time to transport back to get advice from the Guardianship, but that was impossible now. Besides, her heart monitor would reveal something else was starting to happen. She was falling over the edge. It was too dangerous to even consider the consequences, so when the clockmaker returned, she pretended not to notice Gideon's gentle lean toward her. The scent of his body and his heat pattern was evoking butterflies in her stomach and lower down. The physical sensation was thrilling. Now she knew the dangers of getting too invested, allowing her heart to become unprotected. The result would be catastrophic to Gideon, as much as she cared for him.

What was getting in the way of her normal logical thinking, aided by her strong sense of right and wrong and her uncanny intuition, was chemistry. She did not resist when he took her hand under the table. Or when she noticed his breathing was deeper, as she felt every wisp of air he sent her way, infused with his scent, so unfamiliar to her—his former and current angel scent, if that's what it could be called. Not like a human male, something she was used to, but something that yanked her heart right out of her chest. Her ears buzzed and her reason faltered like an electronic device with sporadic power. The internal screen of her future plans and mission was blurring. Music began playing somewhere inside her. She was on the edge of bursting into tears, so exquisite was this feeling of being alive, of connecting with another being in this new way. The music wasn't anything close to a children's choir or chant of devoted angels. It was a full orchestra of feeling with a rich tympani section.

Led like a kite on a string, she sat up straight, chest upright, adjusted her chin level with the males at the table and dared not look at Gideon, though she could tell he was taking sideways glances her way because she physically felt the heat of his gaze. She shivered every time he licked his lips. Her shallow breathing also made it more difficult to concentrate as she felt his thigh press against hers. The warmth from his body was engulfing her, setting her aflame right before their very eyes. Neither Francis nor Manfred seemed to notice.

Did the clockmaker suffer a little reveal, an impromptu smile on his right side after she agreed to take a second glass? It was so hard to tell and anyway, she abandoned thinking about it when Gideon reached across the table to retrieve the vessel, his other elbow brushing against her left breast, moving hard against her knotted nipple. He wove the fingers of his hand inside and around hers, buried deep in her lap, pushing against her belly. She took the glass from him, licked her lips and drank, closing her eyes as his fingers plunged deeper and she involuntarily spread her knees just a few key inches.

There was no denying his need as she opened her eyes slowly and did not smile. He had absorbed every part of her, gentling her shaking frame with his steady hand against her inner thighs. As he pressed against her mound she leaned forward to force him against her harder until it hurt. Her eyes never left his face.

Francis was discussing something with Manfred, which at last caught her attention. Gideon's forefinger touched her pubic bone and lazily circled for a crevice that needed to be filled. The thin fabric of her gown did little to hide the heat and texture of the ribbing on his forefinger or interfere with the delicious back and forth as he probed. He could have stripped her clothes from her right then and there, made her stand or lean back onto the red tabletop and allow him to plunder that place swollen between her legs, even with the two others in full view. The image in her head forced Francis to abruptly turn his, widening his eyes and then searching between the two of them back and forth.

Francis is terrified.

"So there are lots of rules we know about. Guardians and dark angels cannot have relations, for it turns the Guardian dark," Manfred said, casually sucking on a succulent plum, the juice dripping over his chin in a glistening amber rivulet.

Disappointment hit her like a hot spear.

"In your case, Gideon, not that you're thinking of such a thing, I'm not sure it would apply."

Gideon's finger stopped its search, and he used three fingers to separate her legs, his thumb picking up the puckers of her white gown as they efficiently gathered the soft material that was now damp from his persistent movements against her sensitive bud.

Persephone hung on every word of the clockmaker. "We can research this, of course, but I'm fairly sure your vampire qualities shield you from most low-level forms of contamination of the species."

Surely as there is Father in Heaven, this would not

be considered a contamination!

Her gasp nearly alerted their tablemates when his uncovered forefinger touched the sticky flesh of her sex and then retreated in haste, as if thinking further on it.

Gideon slowly moved their joined hands over to his side, once again not looking in her direction but focusing on something on the other side of the room, which caused Francis to turn to check it out and then turn back. Her charge unlatched their fingers, instead pressing her palm against a stiff rod angling up from his lap to nearly past his waistline. He forced her palm up and down along the hard ridge until at last, for no apparent reason, she squeezed him and heard his muffled moan. The timbre was like the growls he'd given her when they passed in the Guardianship halls after his early turning. But the canine sound made her want him to bite her and draw blood.

Again, Francis abruptly raised his head and sported a frown between his eyebrows as Manfred prattled on.

"The bots cannot ever reproduce, even with their own kind," he continued.

"They are just used for sex then," remarked Francis.

Manfred shrugged, adjusting the conversation carefully. "And for pleasure/pain encounters. Nothing requiring euthanasia or surgery, but we do have some in the population below, as in the Human world who cannot feel the power of sexual attraction without causing or experiencing pain."

A gentle pat on the back of her hand reassured her Gideon was not one of those, and she returned him an appreciative squeeze. She began to feel light-headed as the Red-X traveled throughout her bloodstream.

Manfred took notice. "Are you well, dear?"

"I think all the day's excitement has caught up to me. I may be immortal as all of you—or?"

"Yes, dear. I'm an immortal, as well," Manfred reassured her.

"Well, I do get exhausted when I do not catch enough sleep."

Manfred stood up. "I've forgotten myself. Here I told you I'd release you to the company of yourselves and then kept boring you with tales I'm sure you're having trouble following."

Gideon stood, placing his hands on Persephone's shoulders, where she felt the steady beat of his pulse points radiating up her neck and tickling the small hairs below her hairline. "So if I have more questions tomorrow then, will you be available?" he asked.

"I'll make it my mission," Manfred replied, bowing. He inched over to Persephone as she rose, standing closer to her than she was comfortable, but Gideon pulled her deliciously back against his hardened rod with his hands on her waist and hips. Manfred's fingers tucked beneath her chin, and he studied her face, which blushed despite her determination otherwise. "I do hope we'll be able to visit again tomorrow, sweet thing, after you've managed to catch some rest."

Gideon's right hand traveled up her spine, and his fingers encircled the back of her neck under her hair.

"Thank you." She was tongue-tied, vaguely sensing all three males desired her, and it was a strange and exciting feeling. "And I have to find some decent clothes."

Manfred smiled and winked at Francis. "Clothes on a beautiful angel are useless. Don't bother."

Her head was swimming. All of a sudden, the sound of ticking, booming, and tiny ringing filled the room again, sending vibrations all over her hypersensitive flesh. Once again, Gideon was there to guide her, keep her from stepping on a spilled basket of bolts, wire, and strips of copper. The bird swarm was active, but carefully avoided all of them.

"Do they poop?" Francis asked, pointing.

"If they are expiring or malfunctioning. And then you'd best keep your distance because it burns like battery acid."

Francis wrinkled his nose and rubbed his ears

against both of his shoulders, one by one.

Gideon opened the outer door, taking her hand and beginning to lead her through to the freshly washed street. The cool moist air of early morning was refreshing. She suddenly remembered a question.

"Manfred, do I have anything to worry about from those dark creatures tonight as I sleep?"

The clockmaker had now lost his entire former hardened attitude. His demeanor was accommodating, almost overly so. He scratched something at the back of his neck again and then under the overalls in front over his groin area. "Not tonight, angel. You are quite safe tonight. Neither you nor Gideon should attract any unnecessary attention since neither of you are made up of spare parts. I doubt you have a nut, bolt, or screw inside either of you."

Gideon winced while she blushed for the second time. She had a good idea what he was thinking about.

"And what time would you like us to come by tomorrow, Manfred?" Gideon asked.

"Let's say noon. That will give your angel time to recharge and rest. She's a most unusual and delicate creature, and I'm certain you'll want to take good care of her, am I right?"

CHAPTER 12

FRANCIS HAD OFFERED to sit in the second seat, but Persephone would have no part of it. Gideon was grateful, because it gave him the means to watch her face as they traveled at top speed under the colored lights of evening, the ungodly hour when everyone normal and human was tucked safely in their beds.

He couldn't wait to get home, close the door, and be alone with his Guardian.

Every other glance he made in the rearview mirror, she was looking to the side, her face in profile nearly making him stop breathing. Her plump pink lips looked swollen and pouty, and the more he stared, the faster his heartbeat. Francis had been discussing his theory of entering the Underworld and how it would affect them, calculating the chances they could do so without bodily injury.

Gideon was grateful his friend couldn't read his mind since his thoughts were not proper. He was overcome with the images of filling that deep, burning sexual need Persephone carried, helping her body to awaken and take him over the edge with her.

On one of those glances, her eyelashes fluttered over her cheeks as she closed her eyes, bent down as if in prayer. When she opened them, delicate streams of his angel's tears traced down over her upper cheekbones, dripping onto the bodice of her white gown. He knew she was confused, perhaps utterly miserable with anticipation. At least he was hoping that's what it was, and not some regret or Guardian common sense.

He vowed to fix the situation, even if the whole world was on fire and falling around them.

She rocked noiselessly forward and back like she wanted to relieve herself with her own fingers but didn't dare. He gave her a gentle smile, promising to rock her world if she could just hold out a little longer.

"So, there's this transport thing that delivers people back and forth so there is no harm to a non-native." Francis turned to him. "Why does he call it non-native? He said nothing is born there. Everything dies eventually, unless you're immortal."

"Same as earth," Gideon whispered.

"It's run very strangely, don't you think?"

"You mean the lack of structure? It's good old-fashioned trial and error, Francis."

"But you would think someone would take the time to figure it out. Wouldn't that be much more efficient?"

"You've got me there." Gideon studied her again as she adjusted her dress and wiped her tears off her cheeks with the backs of her hands. He wanted those little pink fingers touching him, squeezing him and commanding his manhood to roar to life.

"I get the impression there's more to the story than we heard tonight."

"You are absolutely right, Francis. And that's why our meeting tomorrow will be most important. Help us put the pieces together."

"Right. So, you want me to meet you back here at eleven-thirty then?"

"Meet me over at his place tomorrow," he answered.

"You don't know the way."

Gideon tapped the screen on his dash. "This recorded the route. It will practically drive itself over there tomorrow."

"Handy device. Years ago, who would have ever thought humans would come up with such amazing things?"

"Man searches to figure things out, just like Manfred," answered Gideon.

"Yes, definitely."

They arrived at Gideon's home, and Francis started to open the passenger door before Gideon stopped. The garage door was rolling up in sections in front of them.

"Hold on a bit. I want to get this closed and get inside. I want you to help me with a search of the house before you leave."

"Smart." Francis hung onto the inside of the door as the opening automatically closed behind them all. He scratched his shoulder and once again rubbed his ears against his collar. "Goddamned bots. I feel like I got one flying around inside me like a tick or something. Damn things make me itch."

"I think it's your imagination, Francis."

Francis turned in his seat, addressing Persephone. "You okay, kid? Feeling any better?"

"Yes, thank you, Francis."

"Don't let him keep you up too late, or early in this case, I guess. Something tells me tomorrow is going to be a really big day."

Gideon watched as she ascended the stairway. At the landing on the top, she turned and wiggled her fingers in a child's shy wave. It emboldened him so he raced through all the downstairs rooms, checking windows and stopping to sense heat registers and strange drafts or noises.

"You picking up anything?" he asked Francis.

"Not a thing." Francis glanced upstairs. "She alone upstairs?"

For just a second, Gideon was seized with fear. He traced to the top of the stairs and landed nearly on top of Francis, who had done the same.

"Persephone?" Gideon ran into the bedroom and heard the water running. "Shower," he said and pointed with his thumb over his shoulder.

"Shall I check?" Francis grinned.

Gideon growled, his hands fisting at his sides.

"Okay, I'll check the closets," Francis said, casually walking over to one dark walnut floor-to-ceiling solid sliding door. Gideon took the other door on the opposite wall.

A screech nearly deafened him as he watched a part human, part deep-red-winged creature tumble onto the carpeted floor with Francis and attempt to bite him in the neck with fangs the size of a saber-toothed cat. Something familiar about the expression on the creature's face distracted him until he heard Persephone scream. He left Francis to fend for himself and ran to Persephone's aid.

She was fast and agile, tracing herself out of the glass box of his shower and into the door to the bedroom before the other creature could restrain her. Her shivering, wet, and naked body huddled in the doorway equidistant between the two battling dark monsters. Francis had the same gift of being able to trace but used his skill to pull the death-bringer up by his arms and impale him on the iron spear atop the frame on Gideon's canopy bed. The stake had gone through the creature's heart and in seconds he stopped wiggling and began draining blackish-red ooze over Gideon's mattress, dripping down to the carpeting below.

Gideon pulled the still-struggling creature from the marble floor of the bathroom by his arms and swung him up, bashing him against the glass partition of the shower. Shards of glass were everywhere. Dazed, but still trying to get a foothold again, the figure was slipping on his own blood until Gideon gripped a large section of the plate glass and shoved it first in the belly of the beast, before using it to sever the head.

Turning his head, he angled down and discovered the transformed face of one of the red vampire queen's brothers.

"Fuck me," he swore. He grabbed a fluffy white towel and began wiping his hands of the blood and gore then remembered Persephone was still huddled in the doorway, cold, wet and covered in blood spatter.

She looked to be nearly in shock.

Francis pulled off Gideon's coverlet and quickly wrapped the Guardian and hugged her close until Gideon growled again and inserted himself between them.

"These are the Red Queen's brothers. But holy cow, they're morphed. Deformed. I barely recognized them," Gideon said.

"How many brothers does she have?" asked Francis.

"Dozens. She also has slaves, an entourage." Gideon caught his breath and finally relaxed.

"You can't stay here, Gideon." Francis was not smiling and drilled him with a death stare. Lowering his voice to a whisper, he added just for Gideon's ears, "What happened to her protection?"

Gideon nodded. "I was wondering the same thing," he whispered back.

"All the more reason to get out of Dodge."

"I know it."

Persephone, trembling, attempted to speak. "Perhaps I should go home."

Gideon was filled with panic. "No, angel! Please stay!"

"She's right, Gideon. It isn't safe. If I hadn't been here, you'd have had a hard time subduing them both."

"I'll work on being more in control the next time and call upon all my skills," she said, bravely inhaling and exhaling several times to calm herself.

"This isn't your job."

"I'm your protector," she insisted.

"No. Not when it comes to these guys. This is *my* baggage, *my* past coming to interfere. You couldn't have known. But now I'll be looking for them everywhere."

"And next time I'll be prepared, too."

Gideon rifled through his closet to find some sweat pants and an oversized fleece long-sleeved shirt. He also took the time to complete searching the corners and dark portions of the other closets in the bedroom, finding nothing. He handed the clothes to her.

"I have nothing for your feet that would fit you, but you can wear these pants and top for now until we get you something decent."

She wiped away the blood on her body and then quickly got dressed while Gideon stood between her and Francis to block his view of her nakedness. After she stood before both of them with Gideon's sweatshirt sleeves dragging nearly to her knees, she wrinkled her nose, closed her eyes and produced a pair of boots, in pink.

Francis hit his forehead with his palm. "I can't do

that!"

"I think you can do a lot of things you haven't tried yet, Francis. We'll work on it someday, you and I."

Gideon felt another growl coming on again.

"Deal. Now you need to get out of here. I'll summon some help and we'll do cleanup and disposal," Francis said, looking over the bloody mess at the foot of Gideon's bed.

"Where will you put them?" he asked.

"Best you don't know. Not sure I'm connected to your Red Queen's thoughts at all, and that should stay that way, Gideon. You take your Guardian some place safe and stay there until I message her." He nodded to Persephone. "Right?"

"Yes, I believe we shared some messages this evening at Manfred's," she said without an ounce of emotion.

Francis blushed as Gideon held back another growl.

Persephone placed her hands on Gideon's chest. "We can't go anyplace too complicated, because we have that meeting at noon. I hate to say it, but some place noisy with some background noise would be best. I think that's why Manfred uses his shop to hide in."

"I've got just the place." The look of relief in her eyes was worth everything right then. It also gave him hope. "You sure you have everything under control?" he said to Francis.

"Already put out the AGB, All Guardian Bulletin."

He drew Persephone in his arms, careful to avoid any of the red ooze on the carpeting. "Hold on to me. Not sure about my tracing ability, but I know I can fly."

"As I can," she said, stepping to him and allowing him to envelop her in his arms. With a farewell nod to Francis, he unfurled his powerful dark wings, held her tight and heard one last minute sneeze from his Guardian friend before they were off into the early morning mist. As they soared, he found it no problem to tuck her heated little body close to him, her legs wrapped around his waist and hips, her head gently resting beneath his chin, arms about his neck. He maneuvered, dipping in large spirals both right and left before he realized her own white gossamer wings had wrapped around his back like a warm blanket protecting them both. He thought about Francis's comment and wondered if SB's protection extended through her plumage and hoped it was something they could count on.

The hills were beginning to give in to shades of green from the light grey. An orange-rose glow illuminated the eastern hills and began pouring golden sunlight over the dark bare vines of the nearby vineyards. The Waterwheel Inn was in his sights as he checked the ground below for an unhelpful observer and determined it was safe to land. She adjusted her wings in place slightly slower than he did, like she wanted to continue their warm embrace. She pressed her body against him again and squeezed his wing sacs with her palms.

As she palmed over his chest and upper arms, another long-sleeved white shirt appeared beneath her fingers. She smoothed down the cotton fabric and adjusted the buttons and collar. "There. Love how this looks."

"My clothes overwhelm you, my dear," he whispered.

"I want to keep them. They smell like you, Gideon." She raised herself on tiptoes and kissed him full on the lips, melting in to him.

He resisted the urge to deepen the kiss, drew his arm around her waist, and led her up the stone steps to the lobby area. The night manager handed them a key as if he'd been expecting them. Persephone looked over her shoulder as they walked through the glass doors to the garden terrace leading to the rooms. The sound of water all around them from the numerous pools and gushing fountains was soothing. A lumbering water wheel churned next to one of the buildings that housed a large bubbling hot tub surrounded by stubby white candles.

"You did that?"

He examined the water wheel and the candlelit enclosure.

"With the night manager," she added.

"Ah yes, a little glamour."

"Very effective. Would it work on me?" Her innocent face turned up to him. She focused on his lips and licked her own as they continued walking.

Something in his eyes caused her to inhale deeply and drop her lids for a second. A warm breeze spun her golden hair in a halo's glow about her peachy complexion.

"Wow. Nice," she said without opening her eyes.

She looked like she'd been kissed by a snow princess.

"I've only just begun, sweetheart." He kissed the top of her head and continued up a stone walkway to a set of shallow stairs leading to a veranda curtained off for privacy. The heavy oak door beyond was easily opened, but he had the inclination to walk through the wood just to prove he could still do it, and she squealed with delight as they stood in the warm room heated by one massive fireplace large enough for her to stand in. The mantle was formed stone, chiseled in cherub reliefs. Bunches of grapes and vines were worked into the stone pattern, as were tiny wings on the overweight toddlers depicted sipping naughtily from wine cups.

"First things first. We adjust the shutters."

"But don't make it too dark," she whispered.

He pointed to the fireplace, and she smiled. The bed was covered in half a dozen plump pillows matching the light crème brocade comforter folded back in preparation for their bodies to slide in.

"Shower?" he asked.

"Exactly my thought." She pulled off Gideon's sweatshirt and shimmied the drawstring pants over her thighs.

Her skin glowed from the inside, looking like an alabaster statue hiding a candle flame. Her spun gold hair remained a cloud about her face and chest, obscuring one breast before he pushed the tendrils aside with his fingers and touched her nipple.

She was perfect in every detail, as an angel should be. Her eyes followed his that roamed her body, from her delicate toes to the shadow between her thighs and the perfect orbs of her ample breasts decorated with light peach areolae. Her belly protruded just slightly, plump and ripe. Her nipples knotted as he felt his own erection grow and press against her upper belly and waist. With their thighs touching and her breasts brushing against him, he bent down until he covered her mouth and tasted her need.

Her arms extended up over his shoulders as she stepped up on his feet, then swung her legs to encircle his hips, while allowing his tongue to plunge into her mouth and play with hers.

She moaned. The vibration from her body heated up his soul and set it on fire. She hugged him, pressing her cheek against his, her warm breath in his ear. "Gideon," her gravelly voice called to him.

He held her head between his palms, smoothing over her lower lip with his thumbs. "The first of many, my angel. Your beauty overwhelms me." His voice broke, and for a second, he was unable to speak. Pressing her cheeks together, he licked and plundered her lips again, tasting their soft rosy moistness with flavors of fresh cherries and vanilla. "I don't deserve this."

"I feel the same, Gideon." Her fingers traced the circles around his eyes, and a gentle rain of golden particles descended over his nose and cheeks. "Dust," she whispered to his face's question. "We have glamour and dust, my charge."

She kissed him deeply as the crystals of gold seemed to spread down his chest. He felt tingles on his member, and he broke to look down. Her right hand came between them and she rubbed her thumb over her first two fingers as particles of the golden dust coated him like sugar. Her delicate squeeze engorged him further.

He bent his head and whispered in her ear, "If we don't get that shower now, we won't get one at all."

Her giggle was something new, a lighthearted almost childlike ripple of joy that traveled down his spine. He couldn't remember ever being so utterly charmed, at peace and patient with his desire to love this angel with everything he had.

He was certain it was going to be a religious experience.

Inside the steaming enclosure with double shower heads, their mouths connected again, their kisses extending to necks, shoulders. The side of her face also smelled of cherries, and her hair, done up in a clip, accepted his fingers as he sorted out the delicate strands and let the clip fall, sending her hair back down her back. He squeezed her buttocks, bringing her in to his groin.

The water sluiced between them and over their faces as they kissed in the spray. Her fingers found his wing sacs. She watched his eyes as she delicately traveled up the ridges of his folds, probing and lovingly exploring his angel body.

"This body pleases you, my love?" he had to ask.

"This body pleases me greatly, Gideon. But it is your soul I worship," she said with a kiss above his heart.

"I am completely yours, my angel."

"I give you everything I have, and more when I find it, Gideon."

He chuckled. She was so honest. Being close to her made him feel worthy of the perfect love she sent him. He hoped he could be good enough for her, for there was no matching what she'd shown of her own heart.

They didn't bother toweling off but ran to slip under the cool sheets. Her body had kept the droplets of water warm beneath him. Droplets slid onto the sheets as he placed his arm under her waist, tightening his hold and feeling her mound seek his groin.

Golden light shone from a louver not quite closed, sending a yellow, lighted stripe across the pillow above her head like a message from Heaven itself. He knew it was probably her first time, and he planned to build the bonfire within her body slowly, one ember and one kiss at a time. Again, he peered down into her face.

He wanted to say something but didn't want to ruin the moment, as if nothing he could do would be worthy. Everything he wanted to say he'd express with his body.

She must have sensed his hesitation because she breathlessly whispered, "I'm ready, Gideon," as she raised her head and met his lips halfway. His fingers dove into her hair, moving her head from side to side as she gasped from the kisses he placed from one ear, under her chin, all the way to the other. He loved hearing her breath become ragged. His member pressed into the shallow crevice between her upper thigh and her abdomen.

"I'm ready, my love," she repeated.

A teeny niggle of doubt clouded a little window in the back of his mind as his fingers traveled just ahead of his kisses down the center of her torso, covering both nipples each in their turn. He explored her belly button, that place referencing another life form and time where she had been connected to a birth mother. He said a prayer to whatever angel had brought this beautiful creature into the world.

His lips slid down over her nude mound. He kissed and sucked her nether lips, running his canines over her labia. The sound of her pulsing blood filled his ears, and the blood lust began to return. He pressed her flesh between his teeth gently, not to hurt. But she raised her pelvis to him, begging for something he wasn't sure he should take.

Her fingers played on his scalp, pressing his face

deep into the holy space between her legs. His tongue tasted the dark pink meat of her sex, and he knew from her juices she belonged to him. The unexpected thrill of his tongue rimming her opening and then sliding into her sent electricity throughout his body, emboldening every muscle synapse as he sucked her hard. Her continued pressing against his teeth gave him the permission to again run his canines over her soft labial tissue, and just before he pierced her flesh, he felt the tingle of her dust sprinkled at the top of his spine.

His senses were flooded with music, not heard, but felt. Her angel's blood was sweet and sent a line of fire all the way down his throat. His ears buzzed as he continued to do her bidding. She was writhing from side to side, arching and moaning to the feel of him taking her elixir of life.

She stretched her arms above her head, grabbing for something to hold on to as her arching sent her pelvis deep into his face. His tongue anchored her until he felt her release. He coaxed her sweet juices, licking her wound closed with his tongue, sucking her soft folds hungrily.

Gideon rose above her, one hand grabbing her wrists above her head, clutching them together while his other fingers rubbed the length of her slit.

She dug her heels into the mattress as he kissed his

way up her body, and his fingers spread her lips, satisfying their urge to fill her channel.

Her blooming continued. "Gideon," she whispered. "Angel."

His right hand gripped her thigh and placed it over his shoulder as he bent his right knee and slid his cock into position at her core.

"Tell me, angel. Tell me again."

"I am yours, Gideon. I am all yours."

"Yes, my angel. Say it again," he whispered to her lips.

She tried to speak, but his mouth cut her off. The whispers between them stopped abruptly as he entered her slowly at first, then carefully all the way to his hilt.

Her dust at the back of his neck was delightful and made his engorged member grow. Her moans mesmerized him as he began a gentle rocking motion of his hips back and forth, filling her deeper with each powerful thrust. He watched her face for any sign he should stop. He answered her moans with a gentle "Yes, my angel" as she opened to him, accepted him, and demanded more.

Her eyes opened dreamily. She raised her head, her tongue on the edge of his mouth, sucking a droplet of her own blood lodged there. He tasted her elixir and then felt her own canine make a hard scrape across his tongue. A tiny jab let her suck a drop of his own blood.

He released her wrists long enough for her fingers to find what they wanted: his wing sacs. She massaged them, sending the familiar shivers his seldom-touched parts radiated to the rest of his body. When she opened her eyes he willed the glamour straight to her soul until she arched up and again closed her eyes, followed by a satisfied moan. Her arms and wrists once again stretched above her head, and he held them tight, allowing them to struggle in the pillow above her head. His firm but gentle grip kept them secure while pinning her lower body with his member, drilling home every ounce of desire he'd ever possessed.

The gentle lovemaking continued until he began to stiffen and feel his ejaculation coming on well after he'd felt her shatter beneath him twice. He licked the sweat between her breasts as he continued to hold down her arms, rooting deep inside her, holding her shaking body against him as he came against the walls deep inside her uterus.

Afterward, as they rested and their breathing returned to normal, his thoughts drifted back to that niggling doubt. He'd read about the mythology of angels, fallen angels, and dark angels. He'd not been sure what classification he was, except that his wings were powerful, and black. His body was larger, muscles more well-defined. The rumors about sexual prowess of dark angels came flooding back through that little window of knowledge at the back of his brain like finding a childhood toy. He heard the whispers in the halls of Heaven again. Whispers between the Guardians, with tales of forbidden love and the delicious but deadly fall some encounters would bring.

Alarmed, he placed his fingers above and below her eyes and gently forced them open. He hadn't wanted to see it, but reality was looking right back at him. Persephone's beautiful blue eyes were now black.

CHAPTER 13

GIDEON HAD REMOVED himself to the bathroom, and Persephone figured it was some kind of custom after sexual encounters. She glanced at the light coming through the one louver, got out of bed, and adjusted it closed. Her legs felt like rubber, her ribs ached, and the deep warm delicious ache between her legs throbbed with her new womanhood, if that was the proper way to say it. How would she explain this when she went back to Heaven? To Father?

It was easier to push these dark thoughts away from her to the graveyard of things she'd deal with in the rest of her immortal lifetime. Everything that was important was happening here and now. In this room. On these sheets. In this bed. In Gideon's arms. Her heart became prickly, seeking to attach to something she would be incomplete without. Maybe it was the separation of his physical body, the way his muscles rippled beneath her fingers as he pleasured her, as she hoped she pleasured him.

She dove back to the comfort of the warm, moist sheets they'd created with their long lovemaking session. Gone were her thoughts of self-satisfaction. She became acutely aware she was half of something she hadn't experienced before. Persephone knew she would never again experience being whole without Gideon by her side.

So this was what love was like. The connection. Not just the chemistry of their bodies, but the bonding between their souls. Incomplete without the other, no matter how long she had to endure it. If Gideon were lost to her she knew she'd experience that loss through all eternity. She'd given him that. Or had he taken that? Did he know it would be this way? Would he be forgiving if she felt she couldn't live without him? And what would she do if something ever happened to separate them?

What if he stopped loving her?

She stared at the ceiling, being lit by the bright yellow sunlight creeping along the square corner borders of the louvered windows. Her hand traveled down between her legs, and she massaged the swollen lips his member had caused in the rooting and ramming, and then she touched the bump to the left of her lips in the space between her upper thigh and the soft tissues of her sex. Gideon had taken her blood there.

There was no scar, no open wound, but a bump and sensitivity. Evidence, in case she thought she'd been dreaming, he'd been there, between her legs, drinking from her.

So what did this make her, then? Persephone licked her lips and yes, there were traces of metallic salt faintly present still, further evidence she'd kissed him with his lips still dripping from her angel's blood, and then she'd sought her reward for giving herself, her juice of life to him. She'd taken a drop or two of his blood, and it had spurred him on to a frenzy that left her panting just thinking about it.

Her finger pressed against the bump, and she allowed the dull pain to re-create in her mind that point in time when he took her, when he enjoyed swallowing something she'd never given to anyone before. Not just her sex, her emotions, her love, but her physical body, allowing him to consume her in the most basic sense. She'd even enhanced his experience of it by giving him more and more of her dust.

Persephone withdrew her hand, held it up to the light of the room and saw the glittery gold fall back to her own face and chest. This was proof that she still was an angel. Rubbing her fingers together, the golden sparkles continued to fall. She cupped her other hand, placed a tiny pile of dust there in her palm, then spread it over her sex, and rubbed it into the evidence of his bite. The skin returned to normal. Her labia lost its swelling.

She wondered if she put it inside her, would this perhaps cause another miracle? Could she have a child if this magic were present? If the father became the full force and power of his species and the mother used all the power within her capabilities—could they form a more perfect connection with a child?

It was something to think about.

She heard the shower going and toyed with the idea she could roll over, go back to sleep, and then perhaps be rewarded with Gideon's clean-smelling body hugging her all over again, spooning behind her. Perhaps he'd take her that way, like the books she'd seen in the Guardianship.

At last she couldn't wait to see him again and to see the lust and desire in his dark eyes. She needed to watch him examine her, admire her parts and know the power of her complete abandon to his arms. Without hesitation, she'd take on the whole world if she could just have Gideon's love. And if she had to endure the hell of missing him, the magic of today was worth it to last all eternity.

As she climbed out of bed she shook her head. She

loved the ache in her loins from their physical exertion. She wasn't used to the way her lips thirsted to taste his kiss. Even her hair was on fire. Her breasts felt heavier, the nipples sensitive as she pinched them.

She pushed the door open and soothing steam hit her face. Through the grey mist, flesh-colored shapes danced as she smelled his shower gel, as she saw, the closer she got to the shower, his powerful shoulders marred only by the sacs for the safe protection of his wings. She wondered what it would be like to have him inside her when he unfurled those wings above her. Terrifying, to be sure. But exciting as well. A thrill to set her heart beating out of control, gasping for breath as his head came down to her neck. She wanted the brush of his feathers holding down her arms as she arched up and allowed him to bite her neck.

Was this a foretelling? Was it just an erotic fantasy, she wondered as she approached the glass door and clicked it open? Gideon immediately turned in panic, and then softened when he saw it was his angel coming back, reaching for him, and needing his wet flesh to extinguish the hot flames of her soul.

But he didn't come to her. She went to him instead. He searched her face without a smile.

"Kiss me, Gideon. I am vacant and drunk on your love, and I can't stand it."

The quick closure of his eyelids, followed by a reassuring smile, quickened her pulse. He had been stewing about something. Here she'd thought she knew so much about him, but the lessons learned about him in the last two days were hundreds of years of experience poured into her heart. And still she wanted more.

"Kiss me," she repeated. She pressed her mound against his thigh, then straddled it by squeezing his limb between hers.

His hesitation was brief. He pushed her into the tile of the shower, smashing her breasts into the slightly warm and wet walls. Her fear spiked. But then his fingers separated her butt cheeks. He pulled her backwards to nearly sit on his cock as he rammed it deep. He bounced her, her flesh shaking as she let his thigh carry the weight of her right leg. He angled and went deeper, pressing her again into the shower wall.

She was barely able to get her arm between the wall and her own body, but when her fingers at last reached the juncture where his rod filled her channel, she formed a ring and squeezed him. His growl satisfied everything she wanted. Her fingers found his ball sac. She pulled down and felt the rumble of his chest again on her back as his guttural moan released to the room. His shoulders arched back behind them, his mouth releasing a groan that sounded like pain. Or pleasure.

Or the pain of pleasure.

Instinctively, as her inner muscles reacted to his thrusting, to the sounds coming from behind her, lighting up her spine, she turned her head and leaned, exposing the long muscles of her neck. She laid it bare, nakedly there for him to take. It was a dare to experience the thrill of his fangs pleasuring themselves at her expense. It was a plea to be taken now in the only way she knew how to fully satisfy him.

I'd say that my experience of our sexual encounter was that she was perfect.

The words had slithered down her abdomen, nearly making her sick when she heard them spoken. Some other woman had been perfect for Gideon.

No more!

It would be her mission in life to please him, whatever the cost, whatever the pain. To stay alive to experience the pleasure as he took her.

Her muscles milked him. His cock seemed to expand as she heard another groan. It almost sounded like a muffled *no*. Again, she arched back, lifted her body against his powerful legs and chest, stretching wide her legs, bracing her body on one arm, clutching his right thigh. She dug her nails into his flesh until his skin gave way.

His roar and groan was fierce, and she desperately

angled her head back and to the left, to place her own neck closer to his mouth, which was clearly out of reach. She tried to entice him, to let him know what she wanted because she knew he wanted it. Her lips would not utter it. She wanted to feel it in his roar, in the rumble of his chest and the way he powerfully pumped her to oblivion.

She could move her left hand, so sprinkled the golden dust on her shoulder and rubbed her neck with it, and waiting.

He jerked to a stop. Then she felt his powerful in-hale just before her neck stung when both his fangs ripped into her flesh. He squeezed her left buttock. The pain made her dizzy, but thrilled her. Then he inserted a finger into her anus, and she saw stars until he removed it. His fingers desperately found her bud, and he pressed against it with his thumb while he drank. A ribbon of red fell between her breasts and dropped to the floor of the shower, mixing with the water.

She coated her fingers, rubbed his ball sac with her blood, mixing it with some dust. The large vein at the base of his stem bulged, began to pulse and then she felt the rush of his sperm coat her lining deep inside.

Gideon must have sensed the shiver because he removed his fangs and his tongue sealed her wounds. But he continued to pleasure her, even after all his seed had been spilled.

The emotional toll caught up to her, and at last, she sobbed into the wet tile wall, her heaving chest releasing sounds like a wounded animal.

She *was* wounded. She would never be the same. She was lost in her desperate need of this man, this creature, formed by Father, altered, altered again, and altered a third time by his own hand.

And now he had altered her forever and forever, too.

"Angel, are you okay?" His urgent whisper sent her heart racing.

How could she answer this?

"Angel, oh, my angel. What have I done?"

What was this? *Done? No. I asked to be altered. I begged him with everything I had.*

"Gideon," her hoarseness surprised her. She'd been nearly screaming in the shower, too, and now she felt the constriction, the soreness of her exertions.

"Yes? Yes, my angel? Are you okay? Have I hurt you?" He sounded urgent.

It took every ounce of strength to say it, but she finally pushed it out of her. "Gideon, I want *more!*"

He removed himself and quickly turned her around, setting her on her feet. His eyes were wild with a mixture of things she'd not seen before. Golden flecks appeared in his eyes at her mental begging. "You are drawing my glamour, my angel."

"Yes!" She took strength from his gaze. A fire burned in her belly as he fingered over her bite marks, now healed, on her right side. She drew more dust, crossed over her chest and spread it down her neck and shoulder on her left. Their gaze still locked, she leaned her head to the right and exposed her naked left side to him.

His nostrils flared as the golden flecks grew and nearly glowed. The power from him made her feel like she could levitate, and then she remembered she could fly.

One more pass with the dust against her neck and shoulder and Gideon pulled her roughly to him and with a total lack of control sank his fangs into her neck. She fell against his chest, her palms on his buttocks. She squeezed the flesh of his cheeks as he took her blood hungrily.

She was drunk on the sensation he was consuming her.

"Take it all, Gideon. Take it all."

With that, he stopped. Blood still remained on his lips but his fangs did not show. His handsome face was wracked in pain and then she noticed the tears streaming down his cheeks.

She rimmed his lips with her forefinger, spreading the blood over his mouth and then stepping on his feet, tiptoed, and kissed him, tasting her own blood. When they parted, he was still crying. His eyes were closed.

"God, help me," he whispered.

"Why, Gideon?" Her hands shook his head. "Why? Tell me why?"

"I have taken too much, angel. I have been so selfish."

She was totally confused. She furled her eyebrows together and then shook her head. "You have not taken what I have not freely given, Gideon."

He opened his eyes, but the tears still came as he looked back at her.

"Forgive me, angel. Please forgive me." His head fell against her chest as he dropped to his knees.

Persephone turned off the water and stood, holding his head against her as the *drip drip, drip,* of the water and dissipating steam fell until at last there was a vacuum of sound.

Her fingers massaged his scalp, his temples. She kissed the top of his head, but he refused to let her go, his arms about her thighs, clinging to her like a child, still on his knees.

"If it makes you feel better, I forgive you, Gideon. But there's nothing to forgive. You took what I wanted you to take, no more and certainly no less."

She pressed the sides of his face and angled it up so she could gaze down at him again. "There is nothing to forgive. I am yours, Gideon. Completely. Every part of me."

He buried his forehead in her belly and nodded. "It's time. I have to show you something."

"Okay."

He stood, examined both sides of her neck, adding more spittle to her left side and rubbing it aimlessly.

"Watch this," she said as she made dust in her right hand and spread it over the little bumps that remained of his bite. As she smoothed, the bumps disappeared. She felt rather cocky about it. "Cool, huh?"

It still didn't elicit a smile from him, even after she lowered her head to meet his downward gaze. "What the devil is the matter with you, Gideon?"

He didn't say anything, but took her hand, leading her from the shower. His fluffy towel dried off her body, sifting his fingers through her hair as if it were a comb. With tenderness, he rubbed the back of one hand against her cheek. "My angel. You have caught me defenseless. I am defenseless to your charms."

But his half-smile wasn't filled with the joy warming her insides. The edges of her bright and sunny day began to darken.

"How do you feel?" he asked while he finished patting down her legs and thighs.

"Needy. Famished."

Again, he gave her a half smile. "Are you ready?"

"I told you two hours ago I was ready. I've been ready ever since you took my hand at the clockmaker's table."

"So much has changed in such a short period of time."

"But we have each other, Gideon. We *found* each other."

"And we are changed, my angel."

"Yes. Yes, I freely admit it. I will not be the same Guardian I once was. I am all grown up now. You have healed the cavern in my soul, Gideon. You are what I need. Or is there something else?"

He nodded and held her hands between them. "Yes, there's something else." He kissed her briefly, which left her puzzled. Slowly, his hands atop her shoulders, he turned her body and stood behind her so she faced the large bathroom mirror.

Her attention went to the pained expression on his face as he watched her reflection. His warm body behind her gave her courage and strength.

Until she looked at her own face and discovered her eyes were now black.

CHAPTER 14

PERSEPHONE FELL BACK against Gideon, who had been prepared for her reaction. So the stories were true. Her fate had been sealed. But the most painful thing about it was that she feared Gideon regretted everything they'd done. Instead of a doorway and golden stairs to a life of happily ever after, she'd taken the elevator to the pit of whatever lay behind those black eyes of hers.

Her fever for him hung with her, weakening her emotional shields as he picked her up and laid her on the bed. The morning had jump-started the day. Cars were on the roadway outside the Inn. Birds were chirping. Sounds of water bounced off the stone walls, echoing and magnifying the noise, and cooling her nervousness.

Everything was normal outside her beating heart, but her soul had caved in on itself.

She flashed in and out of consciousness as she

played back the flesh-colored ministrations in the shower, the feel of the sheets tangled around their legs and the way her fingers gripped the smooth cotton bedding. Everywhere was Gideon, bending to kiss her, turning her, bringing her arms up over her head and showering her with lustful whispers and looks as he completed her in every way she could be filled.

Exhausted, she'd pressed herself against his back, and cried, letting herself go. She'd been flying somewhere between Heaven and Hell. Gideon. Her master who had made a slave of her heart and took the only thing she could give: Everything.

The covers were pulled up to her neck. Her arm draped across her eyes to keep them in darkness. The shock of what had occurred eclipsed any question she could form. It was as if the whole world suddenly landed on her chest and there was no air to breathe.

But Gideon was there. Steadfast. Holding on to her so she would know in her delirium, that he was not shirking away from the reality of where they were.

But *who* were they? Star-crossed lovers or doomed fallen angels on a death spiral down into the inky pool of uncertainty? The loss of immortality was a possibility, but it in no way was as important as the knowledge that now she was a burden, something that caused him pain. She was supposed to be his protector. She hadn't been able to protect him from the biggest danger he could face, and therefore hers as well.

His heart beat against hers as he formed a curled shell of protection like a nautilus, his legs entangled in hers, one arm under her neck and the other possessively crossing her waist with fingers tucked in tight against her side. Her deep breathing caused him to fall into the rhythm of their bodies as the hush of heat, regret, uncertainty, pain, and everything else surfaced. Everything, other than hope.

She opened her eyes, not knowing how long they'd been lying there, hoping he was asleep. But she'd felt her lashes flutter against his cheekbone and the corresponding brush of his against her forehead.

"Speak, angel."

She repositioned her head on the pillow, following the familiarity of his face now, forever embedded in her mind, a face she would never stop loving, the face more important than life itself to her.

She rolled to her side, his arm still hanging over her waist, fingers brushing tiny patterns on the small of her back. She caressed his cheek, brought her mouth to touch his lips and planted the whisper there, "What do we do, Gideon?"

His chest filled with air as he thought about his answer, scanning her face again and landing at last on her lips.

"I don't know what we do. I wish I did. But, God help me, I still don't feel like it was wrong."

His eyes were watering and one tear escaped to blot itself in the pillow. His face became obscured by her own tears, turning the vision of his handsome countenance into a watery pool. Her heart was breaking, but there was no turning back now.

"Forgive me, Gideon," she said as her eyes cleared.

His eyebrows tented up and lines deepened in his forehead, the pulsing blue vein at the center sinking into his hairline. His hands pressed her cheeks together. "Nothing to forgive, my angel. I regret nothing for me. But I have taken more from you than I ever deserved."

She placed her fingers over his lips. "Stop."

For several seconds, they watched each other, and then he grabbed her tightly, wrapping his powerful arm around her waist, pulling her to press against the hardness of his chest and thighs, his mouth against hers, commanding she open to him. His tongue searched. His lips sucked the breath and a little moan she uttered right out from her own lungs.

He could crush her with the weight of his body, but she needed his weight to ground her, squeeze all the doubt and worry from her system and make her soft and full of molten love again. With her arms out at her sides, his fingers clutched and woven between hers, she held on to him like the rock her Gideon was.

He was showing her he wasn't going anywhere. His fearless lovemaking lit the match to the promise that perhaps there was hope out there, somewhere.

SHE JERKED AS the small alarm went off. Not sure where she was at first, then she felt the warmth on her backside of Gideon's frame spooned behind her. Their fingers remained entangled as earlier during their arduous session.

The fireplace had gone cold, but the magic was still in the air. Golden particles from her dust floated in the sunlight, moving around in swirls as if by their own power.

"Who gets up first?" she whispered to her side of the pillow.

"You," he answered. "So I can watch your naked body walk across the floor just one more time. So I can envision you coming back to bed and loving me for three days solid." He followed up his beautiful words with a kiss to her ear.

She closed her eyes and concentrated. Slowly, she forced her body to elevate off the bed. Gideon hung on to her, taken by her angel powers until she righted them, landing them gently on their feet with his arms still encasing her.

"Very nice, my angel. I like how you did that. Very stubborn of you, but also very beautiful."

She turned in his arms, resting her forearms against his muscled shoulders, fingers sifting through his still-damp hair. The scent of him had marked her everywhere. She kissed his neck and discovered a bruise there. She quickly pulled back, questioning him with her eyes and rubbing it with the pads of her first two fingers.

"What did I do, poor Gideon?"

"I asked you to."

"But I don't remember! Why don't I remember?"

"You'd had a lot of my blood." He showed her his tongue, with several red marks like well-healed, deep puncture wounds. "It was sore an hour ago."

"I'm sorry. But what are the bruises?"

"You were too careful, my angel. We have to teach you to bite me properly."

Had she heard this correctly? "Guardians don't bite!"

"Wanna bet?" His eyes danced with some dirty stories behind them she didn't want to hear.

"Stop it."

He allowed his tongue to trace the vein at the side

of her neck as he whispered, "Dirty little stories about the things I've done and seen. Sweet little Guardians who made me so hot. You would cream in your panties, if you wore them, my angel."

She pulled back away from him. "Gideon. You play nasty."

"Oh yes, my angel. You haven't seen the half of what I can do. I promise. I can't help myself."

"What would Father think?"

"Too late, sweetheart." He reached and yanked her body to him again as she struggled to untangle herself without using her trace. The struggle felt good. The play was intense and dangerous. Stolen minutes that could not continue forever.

"We have that meeting with Manfred," she blurted as he picked her up and threw her on the bed.

"Not until I fuck you two ways to sunset."

She giggled, throwing her head back as he buried his head between her legs.

SHE CREATED AN ankle-length, long-sleeved pink dress in a light wool fabric and pink cowboy boots to match. He'd already dressed in the jeans and blue shirt she'd provided him, with a navy-blue leather bomber jacket positioned so it cinched his waist and showed off his well-developed ass and thighs, just the way she liked to see him.

He chuckled and pointed to her boots. "You better have socks on, sweetheart."

"Why?"

"Well, if they're new—"

"They're not new."

"Okay, if they're tight and you have no socks on, I might pull the leg out of your hip socket getting them off you. Have you ever worn cowboy boots before?"

"No."

"Well then, we'll worry about all that later."

"Or maybe I'll leave them on all night."

"We could do that, darlin'," he said in a mock southern accent.

"Maybe I'll kick you out of bed tonight."

"Not a chance," he grinned.

"I feel a challenge being laid down."

"Yes, ma'am. We're gonna tumble tonight for sure."

She darted to the bathroom to check her face out in the mirror. The sight of her eyes startled her again while Gideon leaned against the doorframe watching her, fingers riding his angled hips.

"I guess it takes some getting used to, doesn't it?"

"My eyes were already dark before I met you, but in time, yes, you will. I think they make you look more alluring. Less innocent. After some of the things you've done, I have tons of dirty pictures floating all around my brain."

She felt the flush of her cheeks. He walked up behind her, moving her hair off her shoulder to the right. "I want to show you something before we go see Manfred." He lifted the fabric of her dress to up over her rear.

"Again?"

"No, this is something else. Whoa! No panties?"

"Of course not."

"Of course," he growled into her ear. "I like it that way, too. You're a nasty little minx, aren't you? You sure Father hasn't eavesdropped on those dreams you must have been having for years?"

"I don't think I had any dreams like that."

"Honey, I'm sure you've been practicing in your sleep. There's not a doubt in my mind." His fingers continued lifting the dress up and over her right shoulder, exposing her left one. He allowed his fingertips to travel the surface of her flesh until she felt them find her wing sacs. His probing made her wet. She leaned her head against his right shoulder.

He turned her around so her back was to the mirror.

"You see these?" He lightly touched the sacs, which

had puckered and folded up on themselves like her nipples knotted from stimulation.

"So what is it? They're sensitive. I can say that. Maybe more so."

"I'd certainly think so, angel." He inhaled and stepped back away from her. "Unfurl them."

She frowned, not sure what he was talking about. She closed her eyes.

"Wait!" Gideon repositioned her so she was facing the mirror again, but he took two steps behind her, crossing his arms and commanded, "Now."

She obeyed. Her wings had difficulty unfolding and laying out as she brought her arms above her head, palms up, but finally she felt the rumble and friction of a massive set of light grey feathers. The undersides were light rose-colored, which extended down to their tips. She was shocked.

"No more gossamer, my angel. You lost your training wheels."

"What does it mean?"

Gideon admired them, rubbing his hands along the heavy crest where the large cartilage was veined. His movements tickled a bit.

"Beautiful. Never seen anything like this before," he said, not hiding his awe and worship. "And these are way bigger, aren't they?"

"They are. How do they work?"

"We'll try them out tonight on the way over. As for encasing them back, you have to add a little more concentration until you learn the hang of it. But here I am, day three almost, and I'm a pro already. It won't take you long, the way you pick up on things so fast."

He winked at her and again a blush overtook her cheeks.

"Go ahead and try it," he mused.

She lowered her head and furrowed her brow, concentrating.

Gideon stopped her. "No, don't bend your head. Hold your arms like this, like you're holding a large fluffy dog that weighs fifty pounds." He demonstrated and she copied him. The feathers found their homes. She rolled her neck and rotated her shoulders in a circular motion until she felt everything encase back into place and lay flat.

"You got it, kid. You're a natural."

She stared back at him in the mirror. "So, Gideon, what am I?"

"That's what we're going to find out."

CHAPTER 15

T HEY ARRIVED AT Manfred's without a problem. Persephone's powerful rose-tipped wings had helped her frolic in the sky, rolling and swooping down at speeds to make her invisible to humans below. He let her soar on her own while he kept a watchful eye for any unwanted visitors. But he suspected her unique pattern of feathers and color would be eye candy to any other angel: dark, Guardian, or otherwise.

She'd intuitively picked her shade of dress to match these soft colors before she was even aware of them. Her mental alterations while flying enabled her full use of her wingspan and capabilities. He knew she enjoyed the change and the power pulsing in her veins. He felt the same way.

Francis had already arrived when they got to the clockmaker's. They saw him through the storefront windows, chatting with Manfred, examining the many relics and inventions curiously hanging from the rafters. In the full light of day, the various moving timepieces and geared doll parades looked even more bizarre than at night under candlelight. Before they could enter, the outside swarm of mechanical gnat-like insects buzzed them again.

Persephone didn't like them, he could tell. "Don't swat them away. You remember what Manfred said about their parts?"

"Yes. But they are annoying as hell."

"His built-in alarm system. Quite menacing and effective, too. The guy's a one-of-a-kind all right."

Persephone turned the door handle, and Gideon quickly brushed her hand aside and positioned himself to open the door ahead of her. "You have to let me do that, my angel."

She touched his lips with her forefinger. "Got it."

Manfred looked up and grinned, his teeth stained red from his Red-X morning potion. Behind him, Francis's face was pale, his eyes wide, and his mouth gaping.

"Whatever have you done?" gasped his Guardian friend.

Gideon stiffened. "Nice to see you, too, Francis."

"She's lovely. Even more so than she was yesterday." Manfred approached her and took her hand, twirling her around like they were on a dance floor.

"Look at this. Stunning. Never seen anything so beautiful."

His eyes sparkled a little too much for Gideon's taste, and he emitted a low-level growl when Persephone blushed.

"She still blushes like a young bride!" Manfred said, clapping his hands together and disregarding the protest. "You will be battling the minions of the Underworld for centuries, my friend. I hope you're up to the task."

Gideon held onto her hand, squeezing her tight and removing her from Manfred's reach.

"So now what?" asked Francis to no one in particular.

"Now we get our facts straight, and we make a plan," answered Gideon. Francis shrugged and shook his head as he watched Persephone, who wandered the store examining objects.

"Oh, excellent!" Manfred's mood was nearly giddy. "I love planning a big adventure."

Francis's face was sour. Persephone was distracted by a branch covered in mechanical parakeets that were chirping away, some of them forming single word sentences to show off. Their feathers looked like folded pieces of pastel origami paper. She held her finger out to the branch, and one of the birds stepped up to perch there, turning his head from side to side to watch her with both his eyes, one at a time. She brushed his underbelly with her other forefinger, and the bird arched tall in appreciation.

"These are exquisite," she whispered.

"I'd be happy to send you a pair. They are like real parakeets, even do everything living birds do—except procreate, of course. That, I'm afraid, is above my pay grade."

"Yes," Persephone said as she distractedly allowed the pale turquoise bird to resume his position amongst the rest of his flock.

"But they can sustain flight longer than real birds, my dear."

Gideon found this fascinating.

"Well, not to spoil the party," Francis whined, "but I've had a very busy morning. I smell of cleaning fluids, and I've not stopped working since I left you two earlier. I trust you got some rest, because I sure didn't."

Gideon grinned and shared a twinkle with Manfred.

Francis was back to scowling and shaking his head again. "You want to tell Manfred here about our visitors?"

The clockmaker motioned to the back room doorway. "Not here. The walls have eyes and recording devices, and the public can be too curious." He pointed to the shop front door and the *Open* sign flipped to show *Out Of Time* to any passersby. The metal hardware also clicked as if some invisible hand had locked it.

Gideon nearly stepped on Tabby, who scooted around his pants leg, gave a wide berth to Persephone and was the first one to cross the doorway to the anteroom.

A strange smell permeated the room. "What the bloody hell are you making here, Manfred?" moaned Francis behind his mankerchief.

The clockmaker pointed to three new band-aids on his forehead, all three with Disney characters stamped on them. "Wart removal this morning. If I don't keep up with it, I'd look like an avocado—you know, the gnarly kind?—inside of two weeks. I'm working on a remedy."

"I think sometimes the remedy is worse than the affliction," muttered Francis, who then was overcome with a series of sneezes. "Damn it. Feathers. The air is thick with feather hormones."

"I performed a surgery this morning, too."

Gideon didn't want to ask, but Persephone eclipsed his curiosity. "Surgery? What kind?"

"Wing removal."

Gideon wasn't sure he'd heard the clockmaker correctly, but let it go. Francis's forehead was covered in lines of worry. Persephone squeezed Gideon's hand and stood closer.

"You actually do wing removals? Like one at a time?" Francis's defiance to accept the reality of the new world he was being introduced to laced his words, and he sounded like a skeptical teenager arguing with his parents.

"Of course, one at a time. It's a very delicate operation and can have horrible consequences if not done expertly."

Francis would not give up that easily. "Where would you even have the space to do that?" His arm swept over the room, demonstrating all the workbenches and the red table in the center were covered with equipment and spare parts.

The clockmaker polished his glasses on his overalls bib and repositioned the wires over his ears. "Come."

He led the way to a glass door that made a huge sucking sound when it was opened. The trio of angels didn't follow him inside, but hung back and crowded the doorframe.

"This is where the real work is done. I do surgical alterations on request. Sometimes bots need soft tissue repairs on an emergency basis if they've gotten into trouble. I'm a sort of Emergency Room for those who cannot frequent a human hospital, of course." His chest rose with pride. "If I could, I'd spend 24/7 here."

The grey-speckled floor glistened under the sunlight of a large moveable skylight half the size of the room. Several metal gears and chains with various attachments and straps hung in a row on one side of a pristine stainless steel operating table. The place reminded Gideon of some auto body shops where they did motor replacements and remounts. Equipment lined one wall, including a portable X-ray, crash cart, and tanks connected with plastic tubing and face-piece devices.

However, one thing differed from a standard auto body shop. Next to the operating table and theater of wide-angle surgical lamps was an identical table, affixed with strapping obviously intended to hold down an unwilling patient. Attached to the table, a plastic drain tube was still dripping light pink liquid into a floor drain rimmed with a puddle of near-clear fluid. It had recently been cleaned.

Manfred took out two blue plastic sheets and covered the tables, as well as the cart of glistening silver surgical tools between the two tables. He looked up at his stunned audience still bunched at the doorway and smiled sweetly. "All in a day's work." He headed toward them, and they parted like the Red Sea. "Now, let's get down to business."

The clockmaker removed several parts to a life-sized doll's anatomy, including a leg still with a shoe attached, which looked like it had been run over by a train. The leather of the shoe was sliced. The mangled foot and ankle still barely attached with mechanical tendons, and the leg itself revealed different colored wires and tubing at the upper thigh level, as if it had suddenly sprouted worms. He wiped the red table down to a polished sheen and then instructed his audience to sit in the chairs still left from their earlier morning encounter.

"Tell me about your visitors," he ordered Gideon.

"Two of them. Deformed, reddish-brown devils with velvet wings and yellow fangs."

"Did they have a human component?"

"Not much, except their faces. Not at all like how I remembered them."

"And who were they when you recalled what they used to look like?" the clockmaker asked matter-of-factly.

"Brothers. Vampire brothers to a red bitch I used to know."

Manfred's eyes sparkled again. "Charming. She was a paramour?" He quickly shifted his gaze to Persephone. "Sorry, my dear, but I need to know certain things first before I can help."

She gave an efficient nod, squeezing Gideon's hand until it almost hurt.

"Yes, in a way."

"Oh, good God, man. Tell him the truth. Gideon was her *pet*, in every sense of the word. And she was his maker," spouted Francis furiously. "You have to call it by name before you can defeat it. Haven't humans taught you anything?"

Manfred thought this hilarious and had difficulty controlling his belly laugh. "I knew I liked you the first time I met you, Francis. Have you any idea how many of those political types I run in to in the Underworld?"

"Occupational hazard, I'd say," Francis retorted smugly.

"To be sure," answered the clockmaker. "So she kept you. And didn't treat you with much respect, I'm guessing?"

"No." Gideon was ashamed. His voice had retreated deep in his chest, and it was but a whisper. Persephone placed their joined hands on his thigh and gently rubbed it under the table, which made him feel better.

"These guys were not really human," added Francis with a sneer.

"They weren't human at all. They were vampire, at best," corrected Gideon.

"The deformation is from what they've been feeding off. Sounds like they got their fangs into some dark angels, perhaps some disease bots," added the clockmaker.

Everyone turned to him.

"Yes, yes. We have disease bots. Sexual assassins, really."

Gideon swore under his breath.

"Not to worry, my friend." Manfred got up to bring over some fresh fruit and Red-X in a wine carafe. "The effects are immediate. You'd have lots of symptoms in twenty-four hours if your little liaison were with one of them. And they don't generally recall them home, since they fall apart within a few days."

Gideon heard his angel swallow hard.

"And you, my lovely,"—the clockmaker smiled at Persephone—"would not look so glowing, either."

"So, what else aren't you telling us?" asked Gideon on the verge of a growl. The longer he heard the stories, the more concerned he was for his Guardian's welfare, not to mention his own. But that was secondary.

"If she has dozens of brothers and other slaves, she'll use them to drag your carcass back."

"And what about Ashley? The girl? Gideon is really concerned about her," Persephone spoke up.

Gideon developed a nervous tick in his right eye and rolled his shoulder, suddenly feeling pain from an old injury. He'd forgotten what she even looked like.

The clockmaker poured four tumblers of Red-X, but all the angels hesitated. "This is harmless and not nearly as strong as they serve in the Underworld. But the effects will be felt, since you're not used to it up here." He sipped his slowly and continued. "Let me see if I can find a picture here." He rummaged through a drawer in the table, pulling out a thick deck of laminated cards. "Hair color?"

"Red," Gideon whispered.

"Big on top?" The clockmaker demonstrated by holding his splayed fingers to his chest. "Or smaller?"

"Big." Gideon glanced at Francis, who was having too much fun at his expense.

"And lastly. Her special power?"

"What do you mean?" demanded Francis.

"Did you fuck her, too?" asked the clockmaker.

"I certainly did not!"

"Come on, Gideon. I know you know the answer to this."

Everyone was watching him, and he knew he had the answer Manfred was looking for. "Healing," he mumbled.

"What's that?"

"Healing," Gideon said forcefully.

"You drank from her, is that right?"

"I did." Gideon's blood pressure was rising. He was close to dismembering the clockmaker and suspected some of the questions being asked were just for the old man's pleasure and not relevant to the matter at hand. "Is that a problem?"

"Not at all. Made you feel good, like vitamins, didn't it? I mean, you know." He pointed to Gideon's groin area.

"Fuck this!" he said as he stood, yanking Persephone's arm, which brought her to her feet as well. "If I'd have known there was going to be this intense scrutiny, I would have never come. There are lots of things we've all done we're not proud of. Do you have to fuckin' throw it in my face?"

"Sit down, Gideon. I'm not here to hurt you in any way. Just doing my little form of aftermarket research. See, I made your little fuck doll. I was just wondering what the effects were on you, a hybrid. As a made-vampire-hybrid-Guardian-angel-Watcher, you've got a lot of bloodlines flowing inside you. In all honesty, that's going to help you survive when you return home."

"And where is that?"

"I'm sure you realize the only safe place for you is in the Underworld. Your powers will be enhanced. You can take tourist breaks, of course, but here, you'll have many sides wanting to end you. The army you'll need for defense can only be built down there."

So there it was. He was fucked, after all.

"Please, Gideon," Persephone said in her sweet, soothing voice, "Let's sit down and listen to what the clockmaker has to say. There has to be a way. Remember what you told me?"

Gideon cocked his head, at first not knowing what she was referring to.

She angled herself on tiptoes and whispered in his ear, "Regrets?" The softness of her breath and the gentle way she accepted and acknowledged his anger without making him wrong was exactly what he needed.

If Persephone believed in him, the least he could do was demonstrate his belief in that truth: Loving her could never be a mistake. They both sat and gave the clockmaker their attention. "Go on."

The clockmaker held up a card attached with a ring to the rest of the deck. On the slick surface was the unmistakable picture of Ashley. The photograph did not cut off the size, nor the detail of her enormous breasts, since it was taken when she was standing in front of the photographer naked. "This is your little bot," Manfred said admiringly.

He felt the stiffening of his Guardian's spine and her quick little inhale as she examined Ashley's picture.

"Can I see that?" asked Francis.

Gideon turned the card over, but the flip side had a picture of her entire backside as well, the perfect heart-shaped ass and long, flawless legs. Her green eyes shown in profile glowed in the light of the picture flash, making her appear like the mechanical object she surely was.

Why didn't I sense she was a bot, then?

Francis whistled until receiving Gideon's death stare. The card was returned to the clockmaker, who stashed them back in the drawer without comment.

"Just so you know how it works, she'll go back for a recharge and be sent on another mission with her memory wiped. If you run across her again, she'll not remember you in any way, Gideon. Don't take offense at this."

"I don't fuckin' care if I never see her again. That's not what I'm here for. My Guardian seems to overes-timate the bot's importance to me. I merely wanted to know if I'd picked up anything that—"

"Could be transmitted to your love angel," Manfred

finished.

Gideon was about to have another outburst but reeled himself in. "And she's not my love angel. She's the only person in this universe I care for or want to spend the rest of my time with. That's never going to change. My interest is only in keeping her safe. Surviving whatever I have to survive to get rid of the red bitch queen and her minions, and finding out how the hell I can hire that army you talked about for our protection." He looked up at Francis. "I include you in that, too, my loyal friend."

"Persephone could return home," his friend offered.

She squeezed Gideon's hand. "Is this possible?" she asked.

"I'm going to have to double check on that. Not as good with the Guardian biologics as I am with the creatures I've developed. But I'll inquire on your behalf, my dear." Manfred smiled and once again showed his stained teeth.

Gideon allowed his emotions at possibly losing his Guardian to flow through him until they dissipated somewhat. "In the meantime, I've got to keep her safe," he barked. "You mentioned an army. Would this army be able to battle the Red Queen?"

"Oh yes, quite effectively," answered the clockmaker. "And they'd be completely loyal to you."

"So how do I find these men?"

"Warriors come in all sexes, colors, and sizes, my Gideon."

"Sorry, what I meant was, how do I find them? Is there a way I can hire them through you without going into the Underworld?"

"Well, I build them for you, son."

"And, do I—"

"I'll try to make it so you don't have to travel far. But I can't guarantee it. My lab down there is huge, compared to here. Creating an order that size would certainly raise eyebrows."

"But they come *here* and do battle *here*, right?" he asked.

"Yes. That would be best. We'd have less interference. Besides, this army hopefully would be temporary, unless you have other enemies. Do you?"

Gideon faced his Guardian, who was looking to him for his next answer.

"Well, there's the Supreme Being issue."

"And I can't help you there, Gideon. You're on your own with him. I stay away from those fights. But perhaps he'll let you off easy. He can't reach you in the Underworld. It's the only place he can't go. So, if it comes to that, I'm afraid that would be your second choice."

"And Persephone?" he dared to ask.

"A tricky question. I honestly don't know. As I said before, she'd be prized among all the Guardians they try to capture."

"So, I'm still Guardian?" she asked.

"Yes and no. You have some protection in place I suspect."

"I was promised this," she answered.

"You have some of your angel powers, correct?"

"Yes, I can fly. I can heal. I still have dust—"

"For use so you can help Gideon. You forget, the Man himself tasked you. But if your charge cannot be saved, I'm not sure what that would mean for you."

She bent her head, suddenly interested in their entwined fingers again, but Gideon knew she was about to burst into tears and could feel the ache in her heart.

"I wish I could be more hopeful, sweet angel. I'm telling you what I know, and that's all I can do. There are so many moving parts. This is a complicated game of risk and strategy, and we have to execute it flawlessly for an outcome anything close to what you could live with. You must, at all costs, Gideon, save her from the Underworld. That I can assure you would not be good for any of you."

"And the red bitch?" asked Francis.

"You want her as a pet? I can make that happen."

"Hell no! I think she should be burned at the stake for what she's done to him."

"Probably safest. But all her slaves and family have to be eliminated, or—"

"Or what?" Gideon asked.

"Eliminated. I was considering another possibility, but I've ruled it out. No need to consider this. We'll work for total annihilation of her entire clan and all her 'pets.' Fair enough?"

"Can't be too soon for my taste," he whispered. "How will we get them? They're like a pack of nomads, feeding and causing a swath of destruction all over."

"Has she traveled to the Underworld, or do you know?"

"I think she'd like to. Heard her talking about it before."

"Then we'll leave a trap, and use that as bait."

"Perfect!" Francis clapped his hands together. "I propose a toast to this most awesome plan." He raised his tumbler, and the four of them toasted.

"To the clash of the century, then!" the clockmaker crowed.

They clinked their glasses and drank. The cool elixir sailed down Gideon's throat, and he began to hear music that naturally seemed to spring from the pheromones he could taste, feel, and scent coming from his lovely Guardian. It was a cherub choir, something he'd never liked before, but he suddenly felt it was fitting as a sendoff and perhaps a blessing from old SB himself.

But of course, he couldn't be entirely sure.

CHAPTER 16

OUTSIDE THE CLOCKMAKER'S shop, Francis took Gideon aside. Persephone was again distracted by the working dolls in the store window and was out of earshot.

"Gideon, if there is any chance she can return home, you need to let that happen, old friend. I knew some of the stuff the clockmaker told us, but I'm also sure there's a shitpile of information he hasn't revealed. Probably due to time constraints."

"I know it. He practically threw us out of the shop," Gideon answered. "Francis, if I thought she could do that safely, I'd be the first one to suggest it. Though I admit it would break my heart."

"Well, for the safety of your Guardian. I know you'd do it if you had to."

"Yes, in a heartbeat. But this army thing is the best idea I've heard so far."

"Agreed. There's one other thing I'm confused

about, Gideon."

"What?"

"He hasn't contacted me, either. And I'm kind of afraid to request a meeting, if you know what I mean."

"Didn't think about that. With all we've done, I guess I just expected your wings to be dark too, but you're right, you're still a Guardian."

"You think I should just sink back into my normal life in San Francisco until you have need of me? I mean, what can we do until we get more protection?"

"Maybe that would be best. Keep your eyes and ears open, though. Let us know if you run across anything."

"Will do. You guys will be safe by yourselves you think?"

"If we experience anything funny, I'll get her to message you."

"Whatever connection you and I had is now broken, Gideon. Not really sure we had any to begin with, but then, we hardly tried. Wish I had more time with your Guardian. I think she could teach me a bunch of things."

Gideon growled. "Watch it."

"Not to worry, my friend," he said as he placed his palm on Gideon's shoulder. The gentle *tap tap tap* must have released some feather dust because his friend had to bring out the man-sized nose rag. Once again, he nearly catapulted head first into the sidewalk with a fit of sneezing, which drew Persephone's attention.

"Maybe if you flew home, you'd begin to build up resistance to it, Francis," Persephone said helpfully.

"Not taking a chance at that. Can't you see me getting impaled on a church steeple or large electrical tower? It might not kill me, but gawd that would be painful as hell."

"And scary," added Gideon.

"Well, I'll leave you two to make your plans." Francis turned to walk off, adjusting his feathers that had once again become dislodged and had started to creep up from his collar. He sneezed again, and this time kept his mankerchief out.

"Francis, you want us to give you a lift?" she asked him.

"I'm afraid I'd attract too much attention, and I don't want to endanger you. I ride the bus, the trains. I like walking amongst the human population I'm supposed to service. I think I need a little normal human interaction today." At Gideon's wink, he added, "Not that kind, you dirty dark angel."

They watched him amble down the drying sidewalk. Large billowy clouds populated an otherwise bright blue sky. They were tinged with grey. A growling rumble erupted on high. Francis darted a quick look above his head, but then picked up his pace and soon disappeared into the early afternoon. The last thing Gideon noticed was that he was now walking with a bit of a limp. He'd ask him about that next time he saw him.

"Shall we go?" He reached for and held her hands in his, facing her.

"Love to."

"Ladies first," he said as he bowed.

His beautiful Guardian altered her dress, stomped her pink cowboy boots one time, and then lit off for the bright sky, aiming right into a cloud.

Gideon raced to catch up with her and at first he couldn't find her, but finally, through the white mist of one of the larger clouds, he saw elements of rose and peach and at last the soles of her cowboy boots. Her huge wingspan had filled out with more feathers. Some of the rose color had darkened, but the grey remained pale enough to absorb the bright sunlight. He soared above her, showing her his commanding arch and the powerful shiny black plumage she admired. He heard her giggle as they flew over the vineyard across the roadway from their inn.

A small clump of large oak trees had lost their

leaves and defiantly stood on several rocky ridgelines above the vineyards, overlooking the whole Valley of the Moon. From above, it appeared several large pieces of black building insulation had become entangled in the branches from the recent storm. Persephone had picked up speed, cresting over the ridge, and then swooped down, heading for a landing at the parking lot of the Waterwheel Inn just ahead of them both.

Too late to catch up with her, he noticed the sheets of construction debris formed a distinct pattern, rose up, cleared the trees, and traveled in formation like the head of a spear. He sped up, eyes squinting to focus on the shapes when he heard a loud screech, answered by two or three other voice patterns. Distinct shapes formed a circle around his Guardian—who seemed to have trouble evading them with her new wings— faltered, and then began to lose elevation.

But she would not land. As soon as she stopped her forward momentum, the dark beings closed the circle and caught her in the center. Her scream pierced his heart, but soon was drowned out by the cawing and crowing of the beings who had captured her. Their wings were spindly and pointed, appearing more like large leathery bats with a red glow on their underbellies, each with a distinct marking.

Gideon screamed, calling out to her, but there was

no chance he could get there in time as the bulk of the group began carrying her away at record speed. Two of the creatures fell back and now faced him head on, their horned heads down, dripping some kind of dark liquid that was setting the earth on fire wherever it landed below.

He adjusted his speed, backtracked a bit, still keeping the now dwindling shape of Persephone and her captors at the edge of his vision. He corkscrewed downward in an evasive maneuver so the liquid wouldn't light on him. He knew they could chase and overcome him. His only chance was to attempt to land where perhaps he'd have a more level playing field and could use some of his vampiric tracing capabilities.

A blast of fire came from one of the creature's elongated snout. His head was pebbly with black warts and the shape of it was more like that of a reptile with glowing red eyes. Gideon just had enough strength to change his direction and force a landing at one of the koi ponds beneath the slowly turning waterwheel. His instinct had been correct. The creatures didn't follow him there.

He heard their call back and forth, perhaps giving notice to the forward guard that they'd eliminated whatever threat he'd been to their successful mission. As the calling faded, he caught a glimpse of the two flecks of pure evil growing smaller until they disappeared altogether.

He stood in the pool of water, the wheel groaning on its monotonous journey around and around, dumping gallons of water in the pond and over the top of him. At his feet, he saw the large koi that had curiously come to investigate his legs, still covered by the jeans and shoes she'd created for him. As the cool water covered him, he adjusted and enclosed his feathers back into their wing sacs. But just before finishing, he heard a small hiss.

Either it was the effect of water on something that had perhaps been burning in his plumage, or it was the water, cooling down his chest housing his heart now boiling out of control.

He realized for the first time he was no match for the events that would unfold in the next few hours or days. Perhaps he would spend all eternity searching for his lost Guardian, the love of his life, the keeper of his soul, the only reason he had for living.

If it took all the time in the universe, he vowed he'd get even. He'd find her. He'd gladly pay any price to do so.

CHAPTER 17

P ERSEPHONE AWOKE TO the feel of a claw running
up the inside of her thigh. Completely naked, she
kept her eyes closed until all her senses and powers
returned. The bitter taste in her mouth told her she'd
been drugged. She tried to cloak herself in a blanket or
wrap of some kind but found she was unable to.

The claw continued on its deadly course, danger-
ously close to her sex. She tried to elevate, sprouting
wings that jammed into something soft under her back,
but she couldn't move. She was lying on a bed and her
hands and feet were tied spread-eagle.

Snickers and grunts emanated from the corners of
the room. Laughter erupted as she struggled against
her bonds and tried to disappear, but a silver chain
around her neck burned her flesh until she stopped. At
last, she encased her wings and opened her eyes to her
tormentors.

There were four of them, all drooling, with yellowed teeth and lips pulled back into a permanent grimace. Similar in size to the brothers, their faces did not appear human in any way. Their flesh was black and leathery, shiny, and the familiar scent of rotting corpses filled her senses, making her stomach heave.

They laughed at her as she turned her head to the side and retched up nothing. Only a few times as a Guardian she done that, some kind of ancient reflex of her life as a human. She was filled with anger and disgust.

There was no hope, but likewise, she felt no despair. As far as she could recall, Gideon had escaped the creatures. She was fairly certain that if they'd caught him, his burned carcass would be lying in the room at her feet.

The one closest to the bed had long, sandy dreadlocks tied with purple electrical cord. His lips were bright red, stained with blood, and she recognized him as being the one who had feasted on her neck while they flew from the inn. He was bent over her, smiling, blood dripping down the sides of his chin. As his lips pulled back, she was disgusted with his yellowed fangs and horrible breath like the red vampire brothers. He was crouching, one hand barely touched her thigh, and the other was wrapped around his enormous cock as he jacked himself up and down. His sperm sac hung nearly to his knees. It appeared all the energy of this being was concentrated on two lusts: for blood and for sex. Persephone knew she could only endure one of those.

"Pretty. She's very pink and pretty," the creature said as he touched the lips of her sex, which made his cock spurt a creamy light brown substance that smelled like camphor. "I can't decide whether to fuck it or eat it first…"

Persephone retched again and began to shiver.

A massive metal door opened with a screech, and the creature backed up immediately, retreating to the shadows in the corner, his hand still working his rod. He stood next to another creature who had stopped in the middle of eating one of Persephone's pink cowboy boots.

The newcomer who looked her over appeared almost human, well-dressed in black leather, with a cape made from the pelt of an animal. His jet-black hair contrasted with his pink skin where white powder had been applied unevenly. He was wearing eye makeup and blush too. Was that lipstick or was it blood?

"Welcome to my world, my dear." He smiled, showing teeth also stained red.

She didn't answer him, but watched him examine her bindings, kneel at her side, and adjust the silver necklace she wore. The pendant on the chain, which he touched reverently, lay between the two mounds of her breasts. Her nipples were taut, her arms and legs felt the chill of the room and broke out in goose bumps. Or was it the way his cold fingers pressed the pendant to the flesh of her chest and then moved over to squeeze first one breast, and then the other?

He arched back, showing her his fangs, which he brought down into her neck. They pierced her flesh. She heard sucking sounds accompanying his gravely moan. He was famished. His hair pomade was laced with citrus. The powder on his cheeks would no doubt leave a residue. His skin was icy cold yet supple, like the dough of coarse bread she kneaded in the teaching center.

He didn't drain her like the other creature had. Just when she thought she would pass out, he stopped, sat back on his haunches and slurped his lips closed. His hands were devoid of claws, but were deformed and gnarly, and clutched each other as he brought them to his chest. He sighed, and then let his shoulders drop.

"Wonderful. The best I've had." He angled his head as he slathered a look down her entire body. "I love human women, but angel blood just does something to me."

She began to shiver again.

"Oh, my sweet," he said in feigned sadness, knitting his eyebrows together, "Your beautiful little body is not accustomed to our cool rooms of pleasure."

Rooms of pleasure?

He leaned in, a sickly sweet smile spread across his face as he arranged her hair, pinched her nipples, and fawned over the placement of her torso on the bed. His raspy breath was thick with the scent of blood. He availed himself of a double squeeze of her breasts again, and moaned like an alley cat in heat.

Persephone was aware of the tenting in his leather pants.

"I will untie you if you will pleasure me of your own volition."

She remembered Gideon's story of the red vamp. "Never," she repeated his words, finding strength in the knowledge Gideon had fought to the end, and she would, too.

"Um... I also like to take women, force them. Perhaps you will learn to derive as much pleasure as I do,"—he placed his face within an inch of hers, but not close enough so she could bite his nose off—"in time, that is. And we will have all eternity to get to know one another."

So he doesn't want me dead, ended. He will force me, but I will remain alive until I can... can... what?

Seek revenge?

She had never been angry before. She had been schooled never to take revenge on anybody or, in this case, anything.

An idea brightly clung to her chest. She must be in the Underworld, but she was not fully turned. Her wings were still grey and light, not dark. She was unharmed. A prisoner, not a member of the Underworld. Not yet. That meant rescue was possible. She sent out a silent call to whomever could hear her: Father, Francis, other Guardians, but felt it hit something and come shattering back into the room in waves. No one else appeared to sense it.

"My dear, I have waited a long time for this day. If you fulfill your role well, I will reward you with something you have wanted your entire life." He sat back, putting his black boots up on the bed, crossing them at his ankles. The fingers of his left hand traced down from her breast, to her belly button, and then lower, rubbing her nub, a place she now knew well, but which did not give her any sexual satisfaction.

"Let me kiss you there, and I will tell you about your surprise." He blew on her face and yes, a warm erotic wind tickled her nose, soaking into her nostrils and slithering down her spine like a dark drug. But she was still herself. And she still had a will of her own. But she knew, in spite of this despicable situation, she was affected, and it was new.

"I know he has pleasured you. He will do so again, after perhaps I have used you in ways you couldn't imagine."

He? Gideon? She wondered if he was somehow nearby.

"I had wanted you before he got here, but decided that it will heighten my pleasure to have him watch as I"—he took his little finger and slipped just the tip inside her opening—"fuck you day and night until you beg me for more." He removed his finger. "And you will beg me. They all do, in the end."

"Never," she repeated.

He smiled and looked at the black creatures in a row at the sides of the stone wall. "If you can't keep me pleasured and distracted from my awful job here, then I shall have to throw you to them. It helps with the morale around here."

The goons on the side grunted. One was humping the stone wall, pleasuring a large crack.

The human creature removed his cape and laid it over her body. This she was grateful for. "I will take much better care of you than these men, if I can call them that. As you can see"—he waved a hand in their direction—"you could be pleasured by men who like to eat shoes and force themselves on unsuspecting walls." His face looked sad, "They are quite bored, but they'd rather live than end all this boredom, as long as I give them a reason. As long as I give them fresh meat. In the end, it's just a need, my dear."

He tucked the cape up around her neck, arranging her hair again, touching the skin of her cheeks, forehead, and her chin.

"Permit me to introduce myself. I am the Director of the Underworld, duly elected by popular vote. Like all good emperors, kings, and popes, I have chosen the name for my lineage: Luke I." He nodded, hands in prayer formation. "But you can call me 'The Dark One' like you do your lover, don't you?"

She'd never had the desire to call Gideon anything dark. He was master of her heart and everything she could give him, but dark? Do things to her without her permission? Never.

With his left hand, he squeezed her lips together until they hurt. "I love lips, I live for lips. I like lips kissing me… everywhere," he said as he bent over and kissed her. "But, my dear angel, I also like lips to talk back to me, especially dirty things."

A loud scream came from a hallway outside the metal sliding door, followed by the cackling of creatures similar to those that were her audience with the

Dark One. The villains were craning their necks, bending their faces to listen to the metal as if they could hear what was going on on the other side.

"Bring her here so I can show the Guardian how we take care of our women." Her captor snapped his fingers, and the foursome left, returning a short seconds later.

Persephone watched the two creatures hauling their prey into the room, dumping her at the Dark One's feet. Then they were ordered to stand the woman up. She was human. Her dirty red hair was matted and her dress had been reduced to rags, barely covering up her body parts.

As the woman took in Persephone, her eyes widened.

"Please, help me," the woman pleaded.

"Silence! I didn't say you could speak!" the Dark One barked. He scrambled off the bed, walking slowly toward the cowering woman still braced by the grunting and slobbering dark creatures.

Persephone tried to concentrate, unfurl her wings and trace, but again, the silver necklace held her in place, draining whatever power she still had.

Her captor pulled the woman's head up by her hair and sneered. "I was going to demonstrate something, but she's too dirty and roughed up for my tastes." He smiled at Persephone while releasing the woman's hair.

She wished there was something she could do to come to the aid of the young woman, who was surely destined for some disgusting things, but she felt just as helpless as the woman herself. She thought perhaps she might reason with the Dark One.

"Might I make a suggestion, sir?" She was rewarded with a gleam in the Dark One's red eyes. "Perhaps your enjoyment would be enhanced if you allowed her to clean herself up? Or is this not to your liking?"

The self-proclaimed Luke I was at her bedside like a trace. "Or, I could just take the clean one and leave the dirty one to my men."

"And why not have both?"

The woman's cowering stopped. Persephone had drawn the attention of all the evil ones in the room, away from the other woman. The woman yanked herself free of the creatures with one motion, and in a follow-up, took hold of a curved-bladed knife from a pouch strapped to one of the creature's thighs. With lightning speed, she twirled and sliced the legs out from under all of them with amazing strength. The only one left unbloodied and standing was the Dark One himself.

Not Guardian. But something else.

But the woman's temporary freedom didn't last

longer than a few seconds. A fireball coming straight from the eyes of the Dark One suddenly engulfed her. What remained of her was a dark oily patch in the middle of the stone floor after the searing heat.

She could tell their leader was annoyed with the screams coming from his injured accomplices, so after he'd finished obliterating the woman from existence, he turned his fire on the four dark creatures who had brought Persephone to the room. She allowed herself one moment of humor as the large ball sac on one of the creatures was all that remained of him, yet was stubbornly reduced to that scorched puddle by a second blast, annoying the Evil One further.

After his display, he crooned and preened in front of her, a sly smile crossing his lips as she attempted to show fear. It wasn't that hard to mimic, and she did feel her teeth chattering. But she told herself she wasn't afraid. She was cold.

"Better." He picked up a sheet folded neatly in a stack on a table nearby. "This will give you a little warmth. I need my cloak. I shall be traveling the next two days, but I shall return. They are not to harm you. You are to be prepared for my return."

He pulled the cape off her, appreciated her body one more time, bowed, and then threw the white sheet at her. The object covered her as if it had been ordered.

He disappeared through the metal door without opening it.

Persephone closed her eyes to imagine herself in her own bed, walking in a garden, or strolling on the beach with Gideon. She envisioned the bright lights in Heaven, the playhouse and Guardianship classes, and the beautiful sounds of choirs, the Heavenly Hearts radio station with that controversial DJ who made them swoon, especially in her early days there. She tried to remember being a young human woman, and found she still couldn't. Some of the Guardians retained glimpses of their former lives, but this hadn't been the case for her.

Opening her eyes, she stared at the reality of where she really was. The bleakness of the cell made of stone, without windows or light except through a crack under the metal door, matched the sounds of water dripping somewhere and that faint scent of scorched feathers, flesh, and dried blood. She knew there was only one way out. It was by accepting what was real, and making the determination she'd do something about it.

After all, it wasn't about her own safety. She was Gideon's Guardian. That she was also his lover—making her stomach flutter with delight and her spine tingle when she saw his face in her mind—was only secondary to her mission, her job. She hoped that at some point when she had to face the reality of whatever Father had in store for her, paying for her transgressions, that he would at least understand what was in her heart. What her overall intentions had been.

Was it weakness or fate that made her love him? She chose to think it was the latter, that somehow she was destined to be by his side, no matter what the cause. She had never hurt anyone in her whole life, except to defend herself. Surely this must be something another Guardian had experienced in the past. She couldn't be unique. The rumors and whispers whisking around the Guardianship were rife with the fantastic stories of forbidden love and a life ever after filled with joy. A handful of Guardians had been pardoned. But more than a handful were lost. Perhaps her mission was to find them in the Underworld, if she could.

She knew Gideon would be filled with grief, so getting a message to him, somehow, was important. The barrier, causing her telepathic messages to fall back without being transported was a big problem for her. She didn't want Gideon risking his own life to save hers. So finding someone who could carry her message was probably more important than anything else.

She had to stop looking at the moist walls, the crevices where she was sure little insects and unmentionable things were stashed. Screams and groans from elsewhere echoed, chilling the air and shaking her soul. But still, she knew it was her job to maintain focus on the task, to never give up hope, though it was in short supply.

Somehow there'd be a way.

She closed her eyes again, indulging in another fantasy. Gideon kissing her, Gideon in the shower, the way they flew together, the wonder at what had begun to bloom inside her at his touch, the rumble of his voice that thrilled her so. Even the growl he made when he was angry, showing her he would defend strongly anything he believed in, gave her hope for a new day. He was a worthy being, someone who had endured a terrible life and deserved some peace, love, and a future unfettered by demonic influences and other creatures controlling his life. Gideon was a warrior, not a servant.

The music of their whispers and lovemaking warmed her, brought a smile to her lips, and a tear streaking down one side, falling into her hairline. She willed her wings to fluff in her wing sacs, creating a small cushion for her upper back and spine to rest against, giving warmth and softness in an otherwise stark, cold, and damp cell. She pretended they were Gideon's wings sheltering her, protecting her from the elements here.

It was the only thing she could do right now.

I am still alive, and my love burns deep in my soul and sustains me.

That was going to have to be good enough for now.

GIDEON SAT WITH his legs still in the pond, reaching to touch the koi who nibbled salty sweat from his fingers as he waved them through the water. His anger was still there, his heart on the verge of exploding with disappointment and loss, but watching the fish made him realize that no matter what, life would continue, even if the worst had happened to his beautiful Guardian.

He sighed, and then he sat erect, as something in the bushes behind him caught his attention.

The Red Queen showed herself at last, appearing next to him on the concrete ledge.

He wanted to strike at her but found she had glamoured him somehow so his anger was bridled.

"Ah, my poor Gideon. Forever on the losing side, always regretting, eternally running away," she said with her cooing that sent a shiver down his spine.

"I am not running away."

She clucked her tongue and leaned in to him, her cinnamon and eucalyptus scent assaulting his nose. He could tell she was commanding him to wrap his arms around her, but he would not give her that satisfaction. He remained seated, refusing to look at her so her powers were diminished.

"I told you there was no escape. You are my pet. You belong to me because I made you."

"You didn't make me, you *took* me, you bitch."

"Careful, careful. I'm trying to offer you my soothing womanly ways as a peace offering."

No, Gideon did not want to be her slave in any way. He knew she had no soothing ways about her at all. "Everything you touch is destroyed. If you came to end my existence, do so and be quick about it."

"But suppose I were to recall your lovely Guardian? What if I could bring her back from the dead, or rescue her from the Underworld?"

He looked at her, finally. "You can do that?"

"What would it be worth to you?"

"Why discuss something that cannot be done? In all likelihood, she's gone. I failed to protect her."

"Sadly, those creatures did overcome you. But my handsome paramour—"

"I am not your paramour," he barked.

"We'll see about that. Remember, Gideon, that it took six of them to defeat you. What would have happened if there had been just one more on your side? The odds would have been close to even, I suspect."

"Does no good to play with me this way, vampire."

She moved her hand to clutch his groin and balls. "But I enjoy playing with you, Gideon. In time, I think you could learn to like it again."

"That was a time when I hated myself."

"I gave you powers."

"Only to pleasure you."

"And you were not left without pleasure? Tell the truth." She turned with enough angle so that her breasts pressed against his bicep. Her syrupy whisper made his ears buzz. "I ache still for those long nights we burned in each other's arms."

Gideon tried to stand, stiffening his spine and fisting his hands, but the will to get to his feet was taken from him. He was glad he still retained the ability to speak. "I was your slave. Like I said before, you took. I did not give you anything. My own free will was removed."

"Yes, and your Guardian rescued you. Tell me, sweet Gideon, how does it feel to be rescued by a woman? Could you not let this woman do the same?"

"I was not rescued. I was ruined."

"Well, there we have it." She leaned against him. "Allow yourself to be ruined by this woman now, and perhaps I'll give you a miracle."

"I don't believe you can raise the dead."

"Why would they end her beautiful life? What purpose would that achieve? Have you thought about that?" She fingered his ear again.

He craned his neck to push away from her, rolling his shoulder as if he was removing one of the clockmaker's bot gnats. "Stop it. That doesn't work on me."

"Just consider it. I could grant you a wish, and you would grant me mine. Suppose I rescue her, because I have it on good authority she'll be paraded and prized above all others down there. If I did this, would you willingly consent to come back to my bed?"

"Don't you mean cage?"

"For the price of rescuing Persephone from an eternity of Hell? From being fucked and debased, tortured and paraded around until the end of time? It seems like that miracle would be worth the entire world to you. Or would you rather live eternally with the knowledge you did nothing?"

Gideon remembered the conversation with the clockmaker. He didn't want to dwell on it too heavily in case she had some faint chance of reading his mind, so he quickly thought about Francis and one of his sneezing bouts.

"You have evidence she still lives?"

"It needs to be verified. My brothers have traveled

to the Underworld, whereas I have not. But I trust their information. They are seldom wrong, especially with some news that could be beneficial to me."

"I need proof."

"Shall I bring you a limb? A wing? A photograph of an orgy she's involved in? Would that make you feel any better?"

"Stop it with your lies. Your cunning doesn't work on me any longer."

"Because you *think* you have experienced the power of true love. But what is that power if you will do nothing to defend it? Someone who truly loves would try, even if there were the slightest chance of saving her soul. She might not belong to you any longer, but she would be able to live in the light of Heaven again. She would be safe, Gideon."

He didn't want to appear too eager. The Red Queen had given him hope, but he didn't want to show this at all. He needed her to think he was in such despair he was incapable of planning another escape, or some kind of rogue adventure with Francis and the clockmaker.

"Give me a day. I need to consult with Francis. If what you say is true, I want proof, and then perhaps we'll discuss a deal. But only if I have proof."

"And if she is gone, and there is no way she can be

rescued or restored?"

"Then I will join her in oblivion. I have no desire to exist if she is truly gone."

"Very good. Then my task is clear. I give you twenty-four hours. Then we discuss our options, and I will give you the proof you seek, if it can be had. Agreed?"

Her smile was alluring, and she was working hard to cover him with her glamour, but he took strength that he was able to resist it.

He now knew the difference between devotion and obedience.

CHAPTER 18

G IDEON TRACED TO the clockmaker's shop and found it closed. He cursed, which sent the bot cloud into hyper drive, several of the annoying little creatures dive-bombing him, reversing course before smashing themselves into his flesh. He growled and the cloud imitated his sound nearly perfectly. He swore and heard the words repeated back to him in flawless impersonation of his voice pattern.

"Take me to Manfred, your maker. Tell him it's urgent."

To Gideon's surprise, the cloud dropped to the ground and poured themselves under the crack in the door threshold and then flew through the shop into the anteroom door, which was slightly ajar. Tabby jumped to a table in the shop window and sent a pile of books crashing to the floor. Her luminous eyes examined him while her tail wove back and forth like the mechanical second hand on an old clock, stopping several times a second. He made a face and lunged at the window, but the cat was unmoved, continuing her contented stare.

The anteroom door opened. The gnats flew out first, followed by the clockmaker, dressed in a bloody apron. He angrily threw down latex surgical gloves as he barreled toward him, and then yanked the door open.

His hair was disheveled and flecks of blood had lodged themselves in one long stripe from something that had gushed and showered him. His apron bore the same blood spatter patterns. He wore black knee-high boots that were also covered in blood. The tops of them were stuffed with the legs of his overalls.

"Dammit, Gideon. This is most inconvenient."

"Sorry, I have no way of contacting you. My telepathic abilities are gone. I can't raise Francis."

"Yes, well, he's unconscious at the moment."

Gideon looked in horror at the clockmaker. "What have you done, you butcher?"

"A special request. But I'm only half finished."

Gideon tried to grab Manfred by his apron straps but the man was too quick. The gnats were in Gideon's face before he could return his hands to his side.

"Fuck off and come back in an hour," the clockmaker said.

"No, damn you. I need to see Francis. I need to talk

to *both* of you."

"You selfish prick. We've got lots of things to do to prepare. I squeezed in this little procedure, and now I'm regretting ever meeting either one of you. What a pair of self-absorbed and flawed fuckups of nature."

Gideon swiped at the gnats, who stayed away this time, as if commanded not to retaliate.

The clockmaker was going to push Gideon back out the doorway when Gideon stopped him with his shout.

"They've taken Persephone. I think she is either dead or in the Underworld!"

Manfred's expression changed to one of surprise. "How could this happen?" He closed the door behind Gideon to stop a cold blast of wind that had started, swirling dark storm clouds, blocking out much of the remaining late afternoon's sunlight.

"They intercepted us just before we got to the inn. They were perched in a large oak tree like dirty laundry. Six of them."

"Six? Good God, no one could have stopped them."

"Four of them carried her off. I had no chance. They were faster, and they left two behind. Those fuckers breathe and send fire like dragons."

"Yes, the Director's pets. Dumb as rocks, but very deadly. Nearly defenseless on the ground as they can only fire breathe when they fly."

"Well thank you for all that information, but I wish I'd known this before. You might have told me they would be waiting for us."

"And I would know this how?"

"Never mind." Gideon was so frustrated he'd nearly forgotten the rest of the story. "It's worse, Manfred."

The clockmaker stopped his progress toward the back room and turned. "How could it possibly be worse?"

"I was visited by the Red Queen."

Manfred cocked his head and considered this. "She was smart to avoid entanglement with them."

"Meaning she was waiting for us as well."

"I'd say so, yes."

"Manfred, I am just one angel, of questionable pedigree, as you mentioned before. Just one of me. I am nearly defenseless, I can see that now. I need protection, and just where am I going to get it?"

"You want to borrow some of my parakeets? The gnats? Tabby?"

"Shut up and listen to me. We should have never parted. You should have told me what could happen. I would have never let her fly so freely on her own."

"There are some things so basic, I shouldn't have to tell you, hybrid. You are thinking with your cock.

That's what happens."

"Goddammit! What do I do now? I need a helluva lot more than fuckin' flying paper birds and a dumbass cat who might pounce on my shoulders at any second."

"Don't dis Tabby. She'll make you pay. She's very smart. She watches, waits, and gets even."

"Fuck me. Clockmaker, be serious. I am at my wit's end."

"Yes, I can see that." Manfred was at the door to the surgery room and turned to face Gideon with the door in front of him still closed. "You'd best wait here. Have a seat. Let my birds and dolls entertain you."

"I can't fuckin' think with all this *click click clicking*, the chirping and things crashing down everywhere as Tabby explores your shelves of the macabre. So, if Francis is in there, I demand to see him."

"I'm warning you."

"Fuck that. I need to see him."

"Your funeral." Manfred opened the door, entered the room, which was filled with the sounds of opera music but smelled of antiseptic and was as cold as a refrigerator.

Lying on one of the surgical tables was Francis, on his stomach with his face turned toward them, covered in a plastic breathing mask. His skin looked clammy, and he was the palest shade of flesh Gideon had ever seen on a person who was alive.

"You've killed him."

"No, not yet. But if I don't get back to this, I will, or rather you'll cause it to be done."

Manfred pulled back a bloody sheet, exposing Francis's naked back. On the right, his dirty Guardian wing hung down over the table ending with several feet smashed on the ground where it was obvious someone had been walking across the stiff cartilage and veins of his plumage. But on the left, which was the side closest to Gideon, where once a wing existed, a bloody wound had been created, stitched with heavy black twine, puckering to close the wing sac. The wing that had been surgically removed was lying on the ground in a darkened corner, its root covered in dark red blood.

"Holy fuck!"

"He wanted it done."

Francis started to stir, responding to Gideon's outburst.

"Now you've done it. He's waking up. I haven't finished the other side, just got it prepped. You're going to have to hold him down while I get out the straps. He's going to be in extreme pain."

"Give him another dose, man. Don't let him suffer like this."

"I can't. I already used all I can." Manfred traced to

within an inch of Gideon's body. His face was erupting in small green warts, some of which formed right in front of Gideon's eyes. "If you hadn't insisted on coming here without warning I'd be done by now! If he dies, it will be on you!" Manfred held up a scalpel.

Gideon grabbed his wrist and wrenched the scalpel from him, tossing it to somewhere as he heard the steel hit the concrete floor several paces away.

"If he dies, I'll cut you up myself and feed you to the Red Queen and her brothers! I'm not afraid of you, clockmaker. You fix this or your days are numbered."

Manfred traced away from Gideon, standing on the opposite side of the table, his boots crushing Francis's still attached wing. "I'll bind and bridle you if you don't shut up and give me a chance to save him. Now help me."

Francis elicited a mournful moan, which quickly morphed into a blood-curdling scream.

"Francis. I'm here," whispered Gideon.

"Secure his thigh with the strap!" shouted Manfred.

Gideon found the leather belt and cinched it around Francis's thigh while the clockmaker secured his other one.

"Get the one around his neck!"

Gideon looked up at the clockmaker. "He'll choke."

"Or he'll die if he gets undone. Secure him now. See

if you can calm him."

Gideon hated himself for looping a large black strap across his best friend's neck, adjusting a buckle down on the edge of the table. "He's strong enough to fly and take this whole table with him," he added.

"Talk to him, Gideon. I'm going to repair the other one. No time for removal." Manfred brought over the arm of some sort of machine that looked like a dentist's drill and flipped a switch, which began with a whir and a beam of light.

Gideon recognized it as some sort of laser.

Francis was drooling bloody spittle, his eyes rolling back in his head. He'd bitten his own lip. His whole body began to shake.

"Francis, I'm here. Hold on for just a bit longer. We're all here, trying to fix this. You need to remain calm so Manfred can finish—"

"Ah, God, Gideon. End me. End me now. What have I done?"

"Well, you fuckin' should have asked me first. I thought you were going home to San Francisco to roam the city and ride busses."

"Would you have stopped me?" Francis said between chattering.

"Of course I would. And you wouldn't be here on this table doing this."

"And Persephone would be safe now, wouldn't she? Oh God, how I fucked up!"

"Persephone? You know about her?"

"I just got her message. They've taken her! I saw it, man. Just now."

"Happened while you were asleep, Francis," whispered Gideon. "Don't worry about that now. We need to get you right and out of pain. What's done is done for now." He gently laced his fingers through the Guardian's scruffy hair, feeling the sweat and heat of his agony. It was like trying to talk to someone being tortured. His entire focus was on Francis.

Manfred was cauterizing a cut he'd started on Francis's right wing. The smell of burning feathers suddenly filled the room. A single finger of greyish black smoke traveled to the ceiling. Francis screamed, but by the end of the scream, the machine had been turned off.

The clockmaker rinsed the red steaming scar with an orange liquid that further burned Francis's flesh, causing him to scream again.

"We're almost done, Francis. Just another thirty seconds, and I can give you something for the pain. Hold on just a bit longer, my man. You've done good." The clockmaker's skilled hands tucked skin together, stretched the wing sac, wiping the whole area with the orange acid-dipped white cloth. He held Francis's arm, lifting it off the table beneath the damaged wing, extending it outward and bending it slightly at the elbow.

"I need you to try to encase your wing back, Francis. Can you do that?"

Francis moaned, nearly unconscious.

"Do it, Francis."

"I can't feel fuckin' anything on my left side," he mumbled.

Gideon held his hand. "Not this one, friend. Your other one. Try to encase it."

The muscles in Francis's back began to bulge. A bluish buildup began on the left side, but the right muscles began to ripple, where a rosy pink color appeared underneath Francis's pale skin. The wing began to shrink until it got hung up.

"Fuck!" the clockmaker shouted as he jumped to the front of the table, thereby releasing Francis's wing. A few tufts of feathers remained. Manfred pulled on the sac, trying to tuck them inside, but the scar he'd cauterized began to bleed again. He quickly held pressure down on it with the orange rag. Grabbing a pair of heavy shears, he snipped the eight inches or so of cartilage and feathers from Francis's wing sac and closed the flap underneath. He sighed, wiping his forehead with the back of his hand.

"That's the best I can do for now."

Gideon was angry still, but in awe at the clockmaker's skill. It was crude surgery, to be sure, but he could tell the man had managed to save his best friend's life.

He wondered how Francis was going to go with one wing.

"Francis. There, it's all over," Gideon whispered. He continued squeezing his hand and rubbing the top of his head. "You did great, Francis."

"No, I didn't. I failed you, Gideon. I failed Persephone. My fault entirely."

"Stop it. If anyone is to blame, it's me. I was careless and foolish." Gideon looked up at the clockmaker as he continued, "And thinking with my dick."

The clockmaker rolled his eyes and shrugged. He came over to Gideon's side of the table so he could speak to Francis without shouting.

"I've given you a local anesthetic that should help you feel loopy, but out of pain soon. Believe it or not, you will heal very quickly, in a day or two. But I have to bind your wound on the left, and keep changing the dressing. I also have to strap and bind your right wing, which is encased, until we can complete this procedure. I'm going to let you rest a bit, and then we'll do the binding so you'll be able to maneuver about before I leave."

"So I'm a really fucked-up angel, then," Francis mumbled. He drooled over the table, and his eyelids fluttered.

"Unique. I tell my bots they are unique," corrected Manfred.

"Like who the fuck cares about what a bot feels," Francis scowled.

Manfred chuckled. "You'd care if you had one of those pleasure bots sucking on your dick, Francis. Always helps if they think they're having the sexual experience of their lifetime, know what I mean?"

Gideon knew exactly what the clockmaker meant.

"Argh!" Francis attempted to raise his hips, sending his butt a couple of inches into the air. "You fuckin' psychopath. Now you've given me a stiffy."

Manfred nodded, chuckling again. "He's going to be fine. Needs a little rest is all." He grabbed Gideon's arm. "We need to talk."

Gideon leaned over Francis one more time. "Now that I know your pecker's working, I'm not going to worry about your plastic surgery. You rest for a few, and we'll be right here when you wake up, okay?"

"Fuck you."

"Fuck you yourself, you prick." Gideon grinned at the clockmaker. "And if you don't shut up about your stiffy, I'll get Manfred here to put one of those dolls on you, or maybe get Tabby to scratch your back."

"Either one, you asshole. As long as you don't jerk me off."

"Not a chance of that. Sweet dreams."

Francis said something again, which no one paid attention to. Manfred lowered the music slightly, as well as the bright lights and adjusted the heat up. Gideon followed him into the anteroom, and they closed the door behind them.

CHAPTER 19

T HE CLOCKMAKER POURED some Red-X, but Gideon declined.

"So I got one bot service doll here I recently repaired. I say we send her over to the inn to deliver a message for your Red Queen."

"And tell her what?"

"Well, I have to get down there and get your production schedule on track. I've got my crew working on it already, but I have to be there to supervise, or we'll have some kinky shit-like warriors looking more like farm animals and sex toys than soldiers."

Gideon must have sported a strange look.

"I give them leeway, you know. It makes it fun. But I've got an idea that might work. I'd like to take the queen on a tour of the lab. Maybe pretend to be hatching a plan to catch you for her."

"That wouldn't make sense. I'm here."

"Well, I could arrange a pickup. Not 100 percent

safe, but I could get you abducted."

"You mean, like Persephone?"

"Honestly, I think you'd be better off to stay here, but I know I can't make you follow instructions."

"Any other way besides abduction or the transport?"

"Yes, but I'm not telling you yet." He took another sip. "If you go with me, then we'll look like we're on the same side. I think we need to pretend to be enemies, or she won't trust me."

Gideon wasn't sure this wasn't half true.

"Is Persephone alive?"

"Most definitely. Quite a stir down there. Like I said, she'd be most prized, until she's been paraded everywhere for the Dark One to earn his creds."

"What about Francis?"

"He's got to stay clear of the Underworld."

"What if he delivered the message to the queen?"

"That could work. If he'll agree. He has to get her over to my lab first thing. Don't want her running into the Director until I've had a chance to spin my web."

"I think she'd trust that more than coming from a bot she doesn't know." Gideon was heartened by Manfred's nod.

"Gideon, trust me, she knows all about bots. She's no dummy, and she's been around a lot longer than you have. I say we use Francis."

FRANCIS WAS FEELING considerably better by morning when he awoke. Gideon and the clockmaker changed his bandage, double-checked his quickie repair and trussed him like a rib roast so his remaining wing wouldn't interfere with their operation. He reluctantly agreed to the plan, since he was still bearing guilt for Persephone's abduction.

"You give her this map. Very detailed instructions here, and tell her to follow it to a tee or she'll get in more trouble than she's ever experienced before."

Francis tucked the paper into his pocket and finished dressing. His stiffness attested to his recent operation, but he moved quickly enough to avoid any unwanted attention.

Manfred loaded up suitcases of parts and a few mechanical bugs in glass jars. "Nice thing about these is you don't have to put holes in the top for them to breathe. Keeps them silent, too." He held up his array of oddities, stuffed them in a metal footlocker and said his goodbyes.

"Remember, you tell her I've sent a transport for her, so she'll travel safe. I've marked the depot on the other side of your map so she can easily find it. She can take as many pets as she wants to pack in there."

"Got it," Francis answered.

"Gideon, somehow, I'll get you word. Stay out of the Underworld if you can and let me get your army going so you'll have protection. Since they have your Guardian, they shouldn't be as interested now, until they get bored."

Gideon winced.

"Use your vampiric weapons and the little stinger I gave you. We've got a chance. But remember, every plan comes off the wheels at some point, so don't go glum or disappear on me. I may need you to do things up top."

"Agreed. Who minds the shop?"

"Anyone dumb enough to try to break in or get too curious will get a surprise of his lifetime, just before he's eliminated. He or she, I should say. Immortal or otherwise."

"Gotcha. I'll stay away, too."

"That would be smart. One more thing, Gideon. I have the address of someone I want you to contact." He handed him a slip of notepaper scrawled with a name and address. "This guy knows a lot about the Underworld, and the only dark I've seen who was pardoned."

"Who is he?"

"A human."

"So how can he help me?"

"I dunno. Just thought he might have a suggestion or two."

Manfred placed his trunk in a large delivery truck that stopped by the alleyway behind the shop. He secured the locks and whispered something to his bot swarm, which slipped under the threshold again and peered back at him through the glass door as if they were waving goodbye. He stepped into the cab as a passenger and was off.

Francis and Gideon walked back toward town.

"You sure I can't give you a lift?" he asked his Guardian friend.

"Nope. Today I really need to do it this way. I just hope she finds me at the inn." They shook hands. "Hope this works, Gideon."

"Well, I'm going to keep trying until I know the queen's gone permanently. As long as Persephone is alive, I'm going to try to get her back."

Francis nodded.

"One thing, if you run across those dark things with the red belly, Manfred said they couldn't breathe fire unless they're airborne. Just remember that. On the ground they are more vulnerable. Use this if you have to." Gideon handed Francis one of the two palm-sized laser stingers Manfred had given him. It attached to the wearer's wrist with a strap that looked like a watch.

"Wow. Never fired one of these."

"Wish I'd had one yesterday."

"Water under the bridge, Gideon. Hope the clock-maker is able to find Persephone and somehow let her know we're working on a plan."

Francis boarded a local transit bus that would take him to the Valley of the Moon and drop him off at the inn. Gideon considered his choices, and decided to go back to his Healdsburg estate, since he'd not been there since the brothers had met their demise two days earlier. Checking the skies, which remained grey and bulging with storm clouds and rain, he flew, trying to stay cloaked.

Once back in his vineyard estate, he felt safer. Maybe it was the familiarity that was soothing to him.

As he walked through the front door, he could still smell the remnants of the cleaners Francis had used. The place was spotless, and there was no scent of death, or all the blood that had been spilled.

Upstairs in the bedroom, he noticed his shower door had been repaired. The bed was changed, the coverlet removed. Even the area rugs were replaced with new ones he liked. He fell back onto the bed and registered even the pillows were new. No scent of Ashley was anywhere. Nor his Guardian. Nor the Red

Queen's brothers and their demise.

He was grateful for the sleep, which came quickly. He could worry. He could fret and cry his eyes out, but what had moved the universe was so large that he felt powerless to fight it. He needed to rest and rejuvenate, and then he'd go see the human the clockmaker wanted him to meet. Placing the paper on the nightstand, he then changed his mind and left it in his pocket in case he had visitors.

He sighed into the pillows and the soft bed. He'd stopped feeling prepared and ready for the next huge surprise. There had been so many surprises over such a short period of days that, for the first time in his life, he was really exhausted.

And it had nothing to do with sex.

How refreshing!

GIDEON WOKE UP with a start. The wind was still blowing, making the windows rattle. At every bolt of lightning he jerked. The power of the Supreme Being, perhaps his anger, was fully demonstrated. The old man still had it on everyone else for size and scope of drama, like Heaven was the lid on all the action below, controlling everything. Keeping the Universe just manageable enough.

His appreciation for the old SB was improving, he

noticed. Gideon respected that he'd been left alone to figure things out. But he had no doubt SB himself could fix anything he wanted. And it wasn't because he didn't care, it just wasn't his way. He'd have to give it to the Supreme Being. He was certainly consistent.

He wondered if it bothered him his Guardian was captured. Or was it that he expected Gideon would be able, somehow to rescue her? For the first time, he began to see that perhaps there was a plan for him after all. SB wasn't going to come to his aid. Gideon would have to live and die with his own choices and the wisdom of his research.

But there was still so much to know. The only thing left to do was not take her abduction too personally. It had nothing to do with taking her away from him. It was about two things. First, claiming back his life and the seat of his soul. Second, fulfilling his promise to her to protect and be with her for all eternity, or to die trying. If he could keep the anger from what he felt he'd been robbed of from his thoughts, he could think more clearly and capture the next opportunity without being so distracted he'd miss it. His focus was therefore most important, no matter how his heart was aching. That's how Persephone would be, he mused. She'd be making plans, strategizing. That's what she'd learned so well in the Guardianship, where it was taught that everything was always possible. Gideon had never gotten that lesson and always doubted the "Big Plan," as they called it.

He was concentrating on receiving a message from Francis, but that wavelength was still dark. Then tried a connection with Persephone again, and found the same result.

Gideon searched for the paper that had Manfred's friend on it, and decided to visit the man. Locking up his house, he wished he had some gnat bots or a Tabby or two to watch and be his spies, as he flew off to the town of Santa Rosa, not more than a few miles away in search of one Joshua Brandon.

THE VINTAGE NEIGHBORHOOD contained grand homes from the glorious days of the eighteen hundreds, painted ladies with expansive yards and stunning gardens meticulously maintained. The streets were twice as wide as any others in the town. Though the houses were on properties considered oversized, they were nowhere near the acreage he was used to in Healdsburg. Still, it had an order to it, something that looked very normal and inviting. Not a trace of dark angels, red and black creatures that breathed fire and tore angels and other humans from limb. He doubted there'd be a single bot, or at least not one he could recognize.

The front door on Mr. Brandon's home contained a stunning stained glass window, filled with heavenly pictures of cherubs, clouds, and old SB himself, or at least a likeness of him that Gideon thought was fairly accurate. Was this human man protected, somehow?

The gentleman answered his door, sniffing the air as he greeted his visitor. They did not shake hands, and Mr. Brandon crowded the crack in the door, not opening it wide and invitingly.

"I've been sent by the clockmaker, Manfred," Gideon greeted. "He thought you could help me with some of my questions."

Brandon was dressed similar to some dark pirate, his clothes were various shades of grey and black, his boots extended to his knees like he'd been riding. His jet-black hair was pulled back in a ponytail and secured with a leather strap. But it was the man's eyes that were most notable, the darkest he'd seen on a human, almost like he was peering into bottomless pits devoid of any light or color.

"Manfred, huh? I thought that old guy would be dead by now."

"He's immortal. Surely you know that," Gideon answered. He watched as Mr. Brandon's eyes found some sparkle. A smile lifted his upper lip on the right.

"Well, I think this conversation should be held in private, then." He swung the door open to allow Gideon to walk into a massive walnut paneled living room, sporting a fireplace as large as his own. Brandon searched the street in both directions before he locked the door behind them.

"You like some brandy? Or has Manfred gotten you hooked on Red-X?"

"Nothing, thank you."

"Very well. Sit." He pointed to a pair of large red leather chairs similar to his own, sitting across from each other before a roaring fire.

"We appear to have the same decorator, Mr. Brandon," chuckled Gideon.

"These are crocodile. I doubt you have these. I killed them myself, back in my old days."

Gideon was hesitant to sit down on the pelt of a living animal.

"They're harmless. You sit on leather every day, if you drive a car, I presume."

He allowed his fingers to feel the beautiful patterns the ridges of the reptile hide held. "These creatures are miracles. I'm showing respect."

"I deserve some, my good man. They were difficult to trap, and kill." Brandon was testing him, and had already taken his seat, crossing his boot over one knee.

He waited for Gideon to sit before he would speak again.

"What brings you to my doorstep?"

"Forgive me, I'm Gideon, friend of Manfred the clockmaker." He leaned across the distance between them and Joshua Brandon gave him a very firm handshake.

"You are?" Gideon knew Brandon was asking him what species he was without being too obvious in case that had to be a hidden topic of conversation.

"How about you, first?"

Brandon patted his chest. "Last I knew, I was just an ordinary man. I work. I'm an art collector and dealer in antiquities. I live alone and I like it that way."

"Man, as in human man?"

"Yes, last I checked. Do you know something I should?" Brandon grinned.

"And in your former life, I understand you had another bodily form?"

"I try not to discuss my pedigree. Especially since I do not know yours and you come unannounced. I'm not sure if we can be friends, and you said your name was…?"

"Gideon. I am, or used to be a Guardian."

Brandon let his eyebrows rise.

"I was human at one time. Turned to vampire.

Saved to become a Guardian and banished to be a Watcher."

"That's a rather checkered past."

"And one more. I rebelled, so became a dark angel."

"What was the reason you had to do so much penance? Sounds like you made some powerful enemies—in several worlds."

"Not at all. I'm just trying to be me."

"You and Frank Sinatra. Didn't work for him, either. Except the song."

"I actually met Frank Sinatra years ago. Before the Guardianship trip. My maker had designs on him."

"As did most the females in the world. Guardian, dark, or otherwise."

"There are those who have that effect on women. I understand you've had a checkered past as well, Mr. Brandon."

The two paused, staring into each other's eyes without expression.

"Some would call it life. Others fate. I haven't figured it out as of yet. I guess that means it's not over, then." Brandon exchanged boots, crossing the other one and adjusting his torso. "What are your questions, human-vampire-Guardian-Watcher-dark angel?"

"I prefer just to be Gideon. My questions go to the

heart of my description. I mean, I have so many 'bloodlines coursing through my veins' as I've been described, I'm confused."

"Any Father intervention?"

"Not really. Except the Watcher designation. I have a Guardian. A beautiful Guardian."

Brandon was deadly still before he leaned over and stared into the fireplace. When he looked up, his face was telling. "Whom you fell in love with, is that it?"

"Yes. Not proud of it."

Brandon shrugged. "Not sure it's anything to feel ashamed of. Many of them are gorgeous. Their innocence is intoxicating."

"You sound as if you understand."

"Oh, I understand, but as for my own life, I tried to capture many of them before. I was largely successful, too. Redheads. Loved the redheaded ones."

"Ah! The best!" Gideon answered before he could stop himself.

"I turned a number of them before my religious conversion. But I can almost forget how it felt since I have been single for a long time. I take it your experience is rather recent?"

"Yes, two days ago."

"Wow, you got right in there and pounced, didn't you?"

Gideon winced and didn't like the inference. He was sensitive about feeling he was too old for the grace and beauty of Persephone's flawless body. "I am afraid our association has turned dark, possibly deadly."

"Meaning?"

"She has been captured by the Dark One. Manfred is trying to orchestrate a rescue."

"He'd best keep to bot making. Branching out is not suited to him."

"I must admit I think he's rather fond of her as well, although she would never be, well, I trust her."

"You probably *can* trust her, but not *him*. I say this with all due respect, as his friend."

"But I think it speaks to his motivation."

"Just be sure you don't get in the way, Gideon. He is a worthy adversary, but against all the forces of evil in the Underworld? There isn't a being alive, even Father, who understands how it all works. Lots of moving parts."

"As he's said."

"You know that any plan you make will fail. If you succeed, it will be something you didn't count on. It will surprise not only your enemies, but you as well. Trust me on that."

"He's making me an army of warriors to protect us. That assumes we are able to rescue her."

"We?"

"My Guardian friend, Francis, Manfred and me, and his bots, of course."

"You think an army of bots will destroy the Dark One's power? Hardly."

"Perhaps distract him until we can get her safely away."

"You do know the only safe place is in Heaven?"

"Yes, and if I could do that, I would, believe me."

Brandon flicked a feather from the heel of his boot. It was a white one, similar to one of Francis's. "Admirable. Not many could say that. It's that selfish side of being dark, or a vampire, or human, that part that comes out strongest when it comes to moral values. Your Guardian side is probably recessive."

"You're probably right. Harder to be good?" offered Gideon.

"Easier to be bad?" Brandon teased.

"Well, one of the two. Maybe each person is different."

"Very perceptive, Gideon. Well, I think if you have Manfred's help, you have some chance, then."

"Well, there's the other problem. In leaving my position as Guardian-Watcher, I caused a mild catastrophe regarding the Golden Gate Bridge."

"That was you?"

"The one and only." Gideon bowed.

"Quite the statement."

"Probably a huge mistake. I got mixed up with a bot I thought was human. My actions caused me to lose my white wings. But I haven't traveled to the Underworld as of yet."

"And you shouldn't. It will in all likelihood kill you."

"Yes, so Manfred has told me. But to rescue my Guardian, if it comes to that, I must. I will not rest until I have tried everything within my power."

"Which is your problem, Gideon."

"Excuse me?"

"You have no power. Everything you've got is mixed up. I'm sure Manfred explained this to you."

"He did."

"So what can you do?"

"You mean, what powers do I still have?"

"Precisely."

"I can fly. I can trace. I have given in to the blood lust I was denied for some fifty years as a Watcher."

"An enhanced human who can fly, then. No telepathy? You can't disappear?"

"No."

"And your angel lover, did you damage her in your coupling?"

"Her wings are light grey, tinged with a light rose. The most beautiful and unusual pattern I've ever seen. But nothing else that I can tell. She has her dust. She can heal. She has telepathy with Francis."

"Who is this Francis?"

"My Guardian friend I told you about."

"Oh right. Sorry. And he can still go home?"

"Um. We aren't sure. He is allergic to his own feathers. He doesn't like to fly but he traces some. Hates the sight of blood."

"Basically useless. So if Father hasn't called on him, he doesn't want him back."

"I think that could be possible."

"So you have a useless, but convenient friend if he can return home."

"I doubt my answer would be there, Mr. Brandon. I doubt I can myself."

"But perhaps he can intercede."

"Perhaps."

"And he can still communicate with your Guardian? After her *fall?*"

"Yes."

"You have some choices, then, but much risk." Brandon stood. "I wish I could help you."

"But Manfred said—"

"Manfred does not know me now. I don't do rescues any longer, either."

Gideon stood, keeping the three-foot space between them. "So, what would you do?"

"Exactly what I am doing. I'd stay out of it."

"But my love for her—"

"Your heart will learn how to heal. And if not, if the pain gets too bad, you can end yourself. Lots of painless ways to do that."

"I'm not afraid of the pain."

Brandon began walking toward his front door, Gideon lagging behind him. He didn't want to leave. Brandon opened the door and, with his hand still on the lever, turned to Gideon. "You should be. You should be very afraid of the pain, my friend. I wish you all the luck in the world."

CHAPTER 20

Persephone was visited by several female attendants who untied her and took her to a communal bathing area. She was one of several Guardians, she noticed, but she was the only one with grey wings. The area was connected to a large estate with rooms filled with women and some male customers, which made her feel like it was some kind of cathouse.

The attendants were silent, which led her to believe they were personal service bots. Her hair was washed and brushed. She remained on alert as her nails were clipped, her toes painted light pink to match her fingers. She was asked if she wanted Red-X or food, and everything she was offered she refused.

Persephone also recognized there were various types of females in the bathing pools. Some were definitely robotic in their actions. Others appeared human, perhaps angelic, but soulless. Their faces looked gaunt as if some sort of sickness had befallen them. What wasn't present was anything with a fang, or fire, or other special powers. But all of them, except for some of the white-winged Guardians, had dark eyes.

Except for the male customers who wandered in unannounced and pointed at other naked women or stared at her in particular, she might have mistaken this place for a relaxation chamber of the Guardianship. But she kept a wary eye, knowing that looks would be deceiving and at any time the cold dark cells of the prison she'd been housed in overnight would come back. Apparently, someone had been convinced that taking advantage of her cooperation would be more fruitful than having to fight her off. But she was ready for the fight whenever it came.

She heard a familiar buzz above her head and was shocked to find a little cloud of gnats circling. Her first instinct was to swat them away as she'd done at Manfred's shop, but since it was the one connection to the clockmaker, and thereby to Gideon, she decided to bide her time.

The little clicking insects came close to her ear and formed a pair of lips. "Tell her I love her, and I'm coming to get her," came the distinctive voice of Gideon himself. And then they delivered their real message, "Find the clockmaker's lab. You will be safe there."

At first her heart leapt in joy, until the little insects streaked away and left her alone. It could have been a trap, or some sort of psychological mind game. No one else in the room noticed the little horde, and she decided to keep it that way.

She was given a clean white gown with a small pocket over her heart, similar to the novitiate gowns she wore in Heaven. Her feet were bare, and she was unable to produce shoes or slippers, so they remained that way. Gone were the screams, the drafty halls without light and the dank smells of a prison manned by testosterone freaks who existed on pain and debauchery.

She tried to strike up a conversation with others of her lot, but no one wanted to speak, except for one who'd been crying incessantly. While the other angel was being dried, Persephone watched the beautiful redhead's wing sacs being perfumed with oils. Her wings were dark, nearly as black as Gideon's. They made eye contact on several occasions, and Persephone noted her eyes were black as coal.

"You are turned, Guardian?" she whispered when they were left briefly alone. The angel looked down first. Several of the other girls put their fingers to their lips and shushed them. "It is forbidden," one of them said.

The redhead nodded, still downcast. Both of them were brought water to drink and Persephone watched while the angel downed hers quickly as if worried it would be taken away at any second. With her eyes closed, the angel savored every gulp. Then the girl looked up to one of the attendants who were more lifelike than the others.

"I ask you again, when will I be allowed to see him? I was promised I would see him within one day. It's been two."

"Quiet, angel," the attendant commanded. "Impatience does you no good. You wait for the change to be fully completed. Then you are prepared for introduction."

"But I need no introduction—"

The attendant slapped her across the face. "Who and how and when you are introduced is of no concern of mine, nor should it be yours."

Persephone waited until it was safe to speak. "You are seeking a reunion with someone?"

The redhead nodded. "I am fallen."

"So am I. We can be friends, if you like," whispered Persephone.

"What were you promised?" she asked.

"Nothing. I was abducted."

The redhead cocked her head in confusion. "Your lover did not turn you to claim you? He did not promise the lifetime together?"

Persephone shook her head. "I was brought here by creatures of the Dark One."

The angel examined her necklace and her eyes widened. "You stay away from me." She scooted to a corner where she took her place on a padded pallet with pillows, drew her knees to her chest and sank her face into them, sobbing.

Several other males entered the room, each one holding a silver chain with an emblem on it. Persephone looked down to her chest and discovered the one she'd worn while in the presence of the Dark One was still hanging around her neck, the pointed colors of the star pendant tipped with red. One by one, the chains were put around the necks of the others and then all the men left the room. Some angels were inspected first, their skin sniffed and their hair sifted with clutching and groping fingers that squeezed and sometimes touched inappropriately.

One of the gentlemen approached the redhead and placed his chain around her neck. She attempted to yank it off, protesting with a loud scream that caused much attention. The male pulled her arm until she was in a standing position, dragged her into a curtained raised dais, released the sashes to give them privacy, and began to have his way with her behind the creamy fabric. Her pleas and tears did nothing to stop his rooting and grunting, and Persephone was filled with anger. She glared at the other angels.

"You're going to sit there?"

Several attendants headed her way.

"Together, we can stop them," she shouted. She rubbed her fingers together and was surprised to see her dust was still working. She threw it in the faces of the attendants, who stopped, wiping their eyes as if they'd been doused with vinegar.

"Have you no shame?" she continued shouting to the girls. A pair of them also began creating dust, as if suddenly surprised they had the power. Persephone took heart. Three large male attendants entered, and she led the angels to a brief victory, able to send them crashing to the floor with the power of their magic.

"You see, it can be done. We have to stand up for ourselves, since no one else will protect us. But we have numbers." She was hoping her words would find their way to start a rebellion.

Then she was compelled to pull aside the curtain, preparing to grab the curved blade housed in the man's belt, beside the platform, but two new attendants yanked her arms backward. She was pushed into a silver cage and locked in. The attacker inside the bed chamber made a hasty retreat, as the other Guardians removed themselves to the shadows once again, crouching in fear.

One by one, each Guardian was taken away until only two remained: the sobbing fallen angel lying across the soiled bed and Persephone, more determined than ever to save the woman.

After the crying ended, the woman's chain was thrown into the middle of the room. Persephone heard a muffled, "Thank you."

"Do you have any idea what comes next?" Persephone asked.

"I was dreaming of a rescue. You perhaps will fare better than I, since you have the Dark One's emblem."

"Not by choice. He is not my lover."

"I'm beginning to see they lie." She pulled aside the curtain and Persephone saw her attacker had bruised her face.

"But you have someone here?"

"I thought so," the angel said, sadly.

"Do you know the way to the clockmaker's lab?"

"No. Never heard of it."

"If you get a chance, try to get there," Persephone whispered. "I've been told it could be a sanctuary."

GIDEON WAS FURIOUS the clockmaker had wasted his time, and he began to think perhaps it was a ruse just to keep him away from Francis, or stop him from interfering with their plans. This Joshua Brandon was an interesting character, and he obviously knew more than he was willing to divulge, but he also was completely uncooperative.

He began to worry about the plan, and Francis's welfare. He didn't want to be picked up by the Red Queen's brothers, who had an uncanny nose for angel feathers, so decided to trace to the transport station address Manfred had given Francis. He hung on a balcony ledge to a vacant apartment and waited in the shadows. A stretch limo arrived, barreling through a dark hole at one side of a metal three-sided structure, and halted, its motor continuing to run. Two doors on one side and one on the other burst open suddenly with a sucking sound. No one exited the vehicle and likewise there was no driver.

Gideon slouched back farther into the shadows, sure he'd be seeing the queen or her brothers very soon, if they'd taken the bait.

Seconds later he heard screeching far away, not the usual sounds from her brothers, but from dark creatures similar to the ones who had carried Persephone away. Perhaps they were the very same ones. He readied his laser, testing the tiny power light to confirm it was armed and ready to use.

Suddenly, over the top of the very roofline he was hiding under were four red creatures flying erratically with great speed. They looked exactly like the brothers he and Francis had battled. The Red Queen followed and as the group of them touched down on the black-top next to the limo, Gideon noticed they were carrying something that was thrashing in a silver net. Squinting and pulling himself up just far enough to see more clearly, he recognized Francis's disheveled topcoat, with the usual crop of feather detritus extend-ing up his collar. His hands were bound in silver rings, effectively immobilizing him. But they hadn't trussed his mouth and his Guardian friend was leveling a string of invectives so loud Gideon was sure even the SB himself would be able to hear.

The screeching high up in the stormy sky began to get louder and the brothers were attempting to shove the netting into the vehicle. Francis was doing a good job kicking and writhing to make their task more difficult.

"Stop it, angel, or I will end you!" the queen shout-ed.

"I am not invited. The invitation was not for me. The lab director was very specific."

"We have little time. Shut up and get in or I swear you'll be dismembered with your own laser." She held up the weapon Francis had been given. Francis shrank down and she kicked him into the darkened interior. Almost before the last door could be closed, the vehicle sped off into a nearly invisible tunnel that closed up after it swallowed them all.

Gideon's heart sank. This had never been the plan. Manfred had warned him about the dangers of Francis in the Underworld. The silver netting would have contained him, making his wing inoperable. But apparently he also could no longer and suspected it had to do with the fact that Francis was now at half strength with only one wing. He wondered if he still retained his full strength of telepathy and hoped he did.

He flew over the balcony and onto the recently vacated roadway, searching both ends of the tunnel. Nothing moved.

The screeching became louder. Gideon realized the vulnerability of his position and traced through the wall into the vacant building, crouching quietly in the dark. Two dark creatures landed, their long claws scrabbling across the concrete walkway leading from the building to the platform. They barked and cawed, scorched a wooden sign that had been waving back and forth in the wind nearby. Sniffing the air, one of them turned toward the place Gideon was hiding, and headed directly toward him. The creature crashed through the stucco walls and laid a red eye beam in Gideon's direction, the second creature right behind.

Gideon raised the palm stinger and hoped it was at full capacity. He was rewarded with a tiny stream of red heat that seared a hole many times its size in the first creature's chest. The second one backed up onto the platform area and cawed, then raised his head to take flight just as Gideon ran through the hole in the wall to catch the creature's wing, slicing it off with the laser, which sent the black Underworld bat crashing to the ground. Another burst from the stinger stopped the circular twisting motion of the creature, who was trying to get airborne again with only one wing.

But Gideon's luck didn't hold up. No sooner had he put the first bird to bed than he felt the claws of another animal grab him, spearing his shoulder. The pain was so great, he dropped the stinger, which fell to the ground and became invisible as Gideon's captor hoisted him high into the heavens. A team of several other black creatures followed alongside. Another one's claws tore into Gideon's left shoulder and for a brief second he thought perhaps they would dismember him.

His last thought before the blackness crept in from

the periphery of his sight was that he remembered Manfred's words, *So, you'll be joining the Underworld soon, then*?

And just like the clockmaker and Joshua Brandon had predicted, their plan shattered into a million moving parts.

CHAPTER 21

PERSEPHONE HAD DRIFTED off, not aware of it being either day or night. Her ears began to tickle, and she felt the annoying gnats again buzzing around her. They remained in a tight formation in front of her face as she sat up in her silver cage, the bars being too far apart to stop the little intrusion.

As she studied them, she heard the clockmaker's voice, "*Help her,*" as distinctly as if he were standing right there. The cloud of bots repeated the words in Manfred's accent.

"Can you?" she asked the swarm. The buzzing got slightly louder.

She pointed to the lock on the cage door. The little bots went to work, and the lock flipped back and forth, as it was tugged with enough force to even pull the entire cage forward with her sitting in it.

She pointed to the little keyhole on the lock. One by one, the tiny bots entered the hole, causing the lock to begin to vibrate until it exploded, sending metal pieces across the room.

"Perfect!"

Persephone scrambled outside the cage, running over to her fallen friend, who had been chained to one of her bedposts. She motioned to the lock on the chain and just as the cage door had been opened, the bots shattered the locking device on the chain. Her friend woke up, taking swipes at the creatures.

"No. Leave them alone. They are helping us," Persephone whispered.

They buzzed in tight formation close to Persephone for safety.

"Do you know if there's a guard outside?" she asked the other angel.

"I have no idea."

"You are called?" she asked next.

"Rose."

"Persephone," she answered. "Do you know anything about where we are?"

"No. I heard water, perhaps frogs. Crickets? I thought it sounded strange. But I was blindfolded so I didn't see anything."

Persephone faced her swarm. "Show us the way to the clockmaker."

The cloud of bots scrambled under the threshold

and disappeared.

"I don't think they're used to this," she said to her new friend Rose. To the door she whispered, "Come back. Open the door for us."

Next they heard knocking and a dark-suited guard in black leathers, including a mask that covered his whole face and head like an executioner's headpiece, unlocked the door and poked his head inside to investigate the source of the sound. When he spotted the two angels free, he began to shout. Persephone pulled him inside while Rose jumped on his back, sending him crashing to the floor. She grabbed his curved knife and quickly slit the guard's throat and then shoved the body off to a corner.

Persephone stole a ring of keys attached to the guard's belt. "Let's cover him up, make it look like someone is sleeping."

When they exited, she found the proper key and relocked the room. Searching for the swarm, she spotted them rounding a corner and motioned for Rose to follow her.

"Do your wings operate?" she asked Rose as they ran between doorways beneath massive stone pillars.

"No," Rose replied. "I have no dust either."

Persephone concentrated, but her wings did not unfurl. "Shoot. We'll have to go on foot." Then a small miracle happened, she heard Francis sending her a telepathic message of distress.

She stopped to listen to it carefully. "He's being taken to the lab, but he's in custody."

"Who is Francis?"

"My Gideon's best friend."

At last they reached a courtyard bathed in a red glow from overhead lamps. The air was steamy, but pitch black. She followed the little bots as they pressed themselves close to buildings until they came upon a path leading through a garden of some kind. Water was running in the distance.

"Sound familiar?" she asked Rose.

"Maybe. I can't tell."

Persephone squinted since it was difficult to make out the little swarm. "Can't see you," she whispered. Several red dots appeared as the little bugs illuminated their bodies.

"Ingenious. Where are we going, Persephone?" Rose whispered.

"Their maker has a lab here. I've asked them to find him."

Below, they heard music and voices of people who had gathered. Some laughter and whistles like at a sporting event. But the two angels continued on the garden path until they saw a huge metal warehouse illuminated by bright lights with a large circular driveway in front occupied by several large delivery trucks. It appeared to be some sort of construction yard, filled with pallets of material from lumber, bands of wire, and metal tubing. Metal grates and storage bins of various sizes were stacked along one outside wall of the building. The whole area was fenced, but the bots found a cut in the fencing material and bent back a section so the two angels could make their way through without catching their clothes.

The gnats didn't head for the front door, as Persephone had assumed, but formed the head of a spear and tapped against a window spewing bright yellow light over a barren blacktop area.

They heard rumbling of chains from inside as a small roll-up door no larger than a picture window was raised. Inside the warehouse waiting for them was the clockmaker. His black rubber apron nearly touched the ground, the metal helmet with clear visor and over-sized black gloves extending to his elbows made him look more like a welder than an inventor. In the background, a dozen workers were working with saws, hammers, and welding equipment, with opera music playing in the background. They were oblivious to their new visitors.

"Come, come, quickly," he whispered. When he

saw Rose, he stopped her with a glove to her chest. "Wait. What's this?"

"She's with me. We escaped together," Persephone insisted.

"No, no, no. That's not the plan. She must go back," Manfred said.

"Please, sir. They'll kill me. I'll help in any way you wish. Just give me a chance to help save myself."

Manfred examined her gown, which was now ragged and dirty, and eyed her bare feet and muddy calves. He motioned for her to step forward into the light where the clockmaker studied her face. "You are fallen. Who is your maker? You have no chain."

"Dimitri. He was to meet me here. Promised to meet me here."

"She was double-crossed, Manfred. We must help her."

"No, that wasn't the plan and you are not wise to divulge it. Not sure who we can trust, angel. But it's too late." He searched the room. "You both will have to stay very still. I do not want the crew to discover your presence."

"I will not let you down."

Manfred grunted as he lowered the roll-up door behind them. Inside the warehouse there were hanging parts of dolls, toys, statues, wings, and other objects, some looking real, others grotesque like gargoyles. The opera music seemed odd to Persephone, as would a cherub choir. An electric saw buzzed, a nail gun compressor kicked in and several drills were working. Background chatter punctuated with laughter trickled in the air around the industrious place.

"You will have to find hiding places amongst the parts. We are going to have visitors soon. The Red Queen is on her way."

"I felt Francis's message too," said Persephone.

"Francis? He's here?"

"Unless my telepathy has been able to crack your barrier. I sense nothing from on top, so I assume he's here somewhere."

"What about Gideon?" Manfred asked.

"I hope that he is safe at home, but the bots sent me a message from him."

"Hope he stayed away. Hurry, find places over against the wall where you will not be noticed." He cupped a few gnats between his gloved hands and poured them into Persephone's breast pocket. "Send them to me if you have to."

The little bots tucked down into the seam of the pocket and were still.

Manfred pointed to the side wall and the two angels tiptoed quietly to the edge, being careful to stop anything they'd caused to start swinging or tipping over. They each found a stool and sat, using a white sheet draped over one of the hanging dolls to hide under. It was the perfect cover because they could see through the fabric without being seen, as long as they didn't move.

"Thank you," whispered Rose.

"Thank me when we're safe. We've a long way to go."

Manfred returned to the center of the production line and started barking orders. Persephone felt something down at her leg and saw Tabby stretching to scratch her sides against her ankle. The red luminous eyes inspected her, with Tabby's tail clicking in the background.

Rose squeezed her hand. "What the devil is that?" she whispered.

"You've never seen a cat before?" Persephone returned. She put her finger to her lips.

Rose leaned in to her. "Not like that one."

Tabby flipped her head from side to side, sitting on her haunches in front of Rose, appearing more casual than Persephone knew she was.

"Scat, go away, Tabby."

The cat remained and didn't pay any attention to Persephone.

The sound of a door opening and several deep voices entering the room caught Tabby's attention as well, and she ran off to investigate. All work in the shop suddenly stopped. They saw Manfred through the maze of hanging body parts, make his way over to the sound of the front door.

"Welcome, visitors. We have been expecting your arrival."

A female voice cooed something in return.

"What have you brought here?"

Persephone saw Francis being shoved to the ground by one of the Red Queen's brothers.

All work stopped in the lab. The queen's brothers shifted from side to side, scanning the crew, which outnumbered them three to one.

"Ah, I see you have found my lost pet. Thank you, my dear," Manfred said.

"He belongs to me now. I understand you can repair his damaged wing?" she barked defiantly.

"Yes, yes, I can. But then it was I who removed it."

"Why?"

"Insubordination. The angel is a worthless tool, or haven't you deduced that by now?"

"You will fix him for my sister, but she will retain custody," a deep male voice boomed.

The room began to fill with clucking noises and a

few whispers of protest from several of Manfred's crew. Persephone noticed several men had grabbed a metal pipe, a wrench or hammer and formed a small crowd behind Manfred.

"It's quite all right, men. We'll give them the tour, and then send them on their way. If you insist, you can keep your pet."

Francis moaned in response to the sound of someone's boot kicking him.

"You mistreat a pet and they will turn on you, Queen. Even in the Underworld there are rules of conduct."

She scoffed. The sounds of her little feet stepping on the gritty concrete floor echoed throughout the room. No one else made a sound.

"So you are building a doll, Special Forces I see?" she said with disgust. "An army of dolls. And for whom?"

Persephone could see her bright burgundy cape flowing about her thin body like a veil of smoke. She was sure it was some sort of protection device and apparently it worked in the Underworld.

"A new contract, Queen."

"For whom? Answer me," she barked.

"We are building several new bots."

"Why?"

"Because it was contracted and hired." Manfred's voice was becoming strained. Persephone felt the bugs in her pocket becoming agitated.

"You work for Guardians and Watchers now, clockmaker? And why do they call you clockmaker when you make dolls?"

"Warrior dolls. Special bots for various purposes. Some for pleasure. Some for pain. Which is your preference?"

"I wish to own the warriors Francis said you are building."

"These?" The clockmaker tried to make it look like a joke. "These are harmless. I could build others for you. Perhaps even more enhanced. Your specifications and tastes."

Somewhere in the shop a tool dropped and Persephone felt tension rise in the room. The red vamp quickly turned in that direction. "What is it that moves over there?"

Manfred stood beside her. "That's my cat."

"That's not a cat."

"You are mistaken, my dear. That is my cat, Tabby. I take very good care my Tabby." He bent down. "Come here Tabby, show yourself."

The sound of the cat's paws were so light Persephone had a hard time hearing anything at all. Rose's face was squinting to watch what was going on. They watched Manfred pick Tabby up and present her to the red vamp.

"Fascinating, but ugly as hell," she said as she took the animal, cradling her in her arms. "That tail is disgusting and," the Queen leaned over to sniff the non-existent fur, which Persephone knew was a huge mistake, "she smells horrible." The Queen was going to toss her, but before she could, Tabby reared back and flung herself onto the vamp's face, digging her claws into her flesh. The vamp screamed, shattering one of the skylights. Pieces of glass fell into the room like rain.

The workforce began to grumble as the queen's brothers sprang into action, attempting to remove the cat from her face and neck. One by one, they were repelled. Large arcs of blood sprayed in several directions as the cat's claws had success with the devilish vamp brothers' flesh.

Manfred shouted, "Outrage! You disrespect our work here and you shall pay!"

This signaled the crew, who moved into action, creating a fray resulting in parts flying and crashing to the ground, bodies of workmen as well as parts of the brothers flew and landed limp on table tops, pieces of sinew and strings of gut dripping blood on innocent-looking doll faces.

In the commotion, Manfred hauled Francis up and shoved him in their direction. Persephone caught the Guardian and held him tight. "Thank goodness you're okay."

He returned the hug and then stared back between the two angels. "How did you get here?"

Persephone put her finger to her lips again. Rose handed Francis her palm and whispered, "I'm Rose, fallen angel."

"Francis, broken angel, friend," he whispered in return. He turned to Persephone, ducking to avoid being hit by a metal wrench that had flown just over the top of his head. "You got my messages, then."

"Yes. I hope soon we can leave. I worry about leaving Gideon up top on his own."

"Not soon enough, angel."

"Should we help them?" she asked.

Before she got an answer, she ran to the Red Queen, and threw dust she'd been collecting in her pocket, right into the vamp's face. Tabby had scrambled off somewhere, but as the dust hit her, she fell backward.

Thinking quickly, she decided to try something she'd been considering. Holding the Red Queen's forearm, she picked up the arm of one of her unconscious brothers and held the two limbs together. White light confirmed that the healing would occur, but the bones, and flesh would be fused. She left the queen kicking her brother, trying to wake him, as his dead weight made it impossible for her to fight.

One of the other brothers was starting to elevate. Manfred shouted to Francis, who came running from the corner, and pulled the beast down, and hit his skull with a hammer.

It took several minutes for the fight to subside. The three angels waited at the edge of the fight, until they were convinced Manfred's side had won.

Manfred approached, bloody, but sporting a grin from ear to ear. "We recycle everything here because it is so difficult to get material. It all has to be shipped in. Do you suppose Gideon will mind if part of his army is made up of some spare parts we managed to procure this evening?"

Persephone stood in shock at the mayhem.

"My dear, if you ever change your mind about living down here, I could certainly use your quick-thinking skills.

From under a table, Tabby strutted proudly, chewing a part of a red leather wing.

CHAPTER 22

GIDEON LAY IN the cold cell by himself. His shoulders were swollen, his body burning up with fever from the infection started by the fouled claws of the winged creatures that had carried him to the Underworld. He was not healing, would probably never heal here, and in all likelihood would die soon.

Good riddance.

He'd failed again. Failed to adequately protect Persephone, and his friend Francis, and possibly plunged his other more distant friend, the genius clockmaker who had also risked it all to try to support the rescue, into an eternity of pain and suffering.

He only hoped that some of the Red Queen's brothers had somehow found a fiery grave somewhere. The guards had told him the angel who had been held for the Director had fought back, sliced the legs from their fellow guards and met her end by the Director's fireball. They said his beautiful angel flamed blue, and then was reduced to an oily spot on the ground.

He told himself he should have more hope, but he was tired, weakened by fighting, exhausted from looking over his shoulder for enemies. Tired of losing. Tired of finding brief glimpses of joy packed on all sides with confusion, heartache, and despair.

Even if he survived the death camp he was destined for, escaped the Underworld to be able to crawl around the human world in his deformed state, there was still one more confrontation he would not be able to avoid. And he'd deserve whatever the old SB would bring him.

His one regret was that he'd been unable to say goodbye to her. The bots had been dispatched to deliver his message of love to his lovely Guardian after the poor angel had been destroyed. Everything was too little, too late. Everything was over.

He willed the infection to rage further. His anger raised his blood pressure higher. The heart beating inside his chest was erratic, and he was forcing it to run off the rails. He was done with the suffering.

It irritated him the clockmaker had made a point to mention Gideon had given up when he'd chucked his Watcher life on top of the bridge. That day seemed so long ago, and yet it had been barely a week, and now the Universe had turned on its axis.

But once again, he was failing. Failing to die a good, clean, fast death. A death in combat, fighting for the honor and love of his beloved. No, he'd die from a sickly infection he was too weak to overcome. Being a freak of nature had finally caught up to him. He felt like he was coming apart like one of the clockmaker's bots.

The air was foul. The dripping walls were disgusting. He could hear little animals trying to find some shelter from the doom and gloom. Even insects and earth bugs could find no refuge.

If he raised a stink, perhaps they'd end him quickly. If he could enrage them, perhaps they'd beat him to death. It was far better than rotting away, forgotten, and alone. With difficulty, he sat up, leaned his back against the wall, and attempted to use his wings as cushion and perhaps cover, but the wings stayed stubbornly encased just as if they'd been sewn shut.

He inhaled and let out a roar that shook the building. He roared again as the visions of his life flashed before him, all the things he soon would no longer pine for, but things nonetheless be forever denied. Failure was such a bitter pill. He wanted the chance to join his angel if that was even possible.

He reached out to Francis, though their connection had been broken some time ago.

Tell her I loved her when you see her. Tell her I regret so that she cannot return to Heaven where she'd be safe. Ask for forgiveness from her beautiful heart, her bottomless soul.

Of course, he got no response. That's because Francis was probably also dead. He'd be leaving his parting message for the stones digging into his backside.

Again, he roared because it was the only thing he could do. He thought maybe if he was so loud, perhaps it would send his voice clear through to the human world above, and perhaps beyond, if it were possible. Perhaps he'd cause an earthquake. But no further rumbling lingered after his last outburst.

He was done.

Come take me. Bury me.

PERSEPHONE AND ROSE were seated in the back of the large delivery truck, hidden under tarps thrown over metal storage lockers. Manfred insisted on being driver and Francis was his co-pilot. The fallen angels had heard him give instructions for the cleanup to hide their mini war with the Red Queen and her brothers. It had been a Red-Letter day for the crew, who were eager to put it past them, use the body parts and experiment with warrior making. The room had been buzzing with energy.

She heard the engine start and the truck began traveling down the bumpy road Manfred mentioned was the back door to the Underworld, a place where deliveries were taken and removed. Only a handful of people knew about this access, he'd told them.

As they'd pulled away she thought she'd heard a scream coming from down below. She banged on the side of the metal but Manfred hadn't paid attention, or didn't hear her. She listened again and heard the distinctive mournful howl that could only come from one being in the universe: Gideon.

"Do you hear it?" she asked Rose.

"Sounds like someone being tortured. I will be so happy to get away from all this bleakness, this death and darkness."

But Persephone wouldn't be convinced it was just some anonymous cry for help. She felt the vibration in her heart that he was in pain, and that they were about to leave him behind.

That was unacceptable.

She stood, banging on the back of the cab, shouting for the clockmaker to stop. Then she sent a telepathic message to Francis, cursing herself that she hadn't used that earlier.

The truck stopped. Soon Manfred opened the massive metal doors at the rear and stared into the van.

Francis was standing next to him.

"You are sure, angel? You are sure it's him?" Francis asked.

"Not a doubt in my mind."

Manfred was swearing. "Not safe. This is not safe. We are ready to make a clean getaway, and you risk it all by turning back now, Persephone."

"Then you go on, and I'll go back alone. But I will not leave this place until I find out if he's still here. I alone shall pay the price then if I'm wrong."

"Send the bots, Manfred," Francis said urgently, "Let them find Gideon and deliver back a message."

"We shouldn't wait."

Persephone jumped out of the van and began running back on foot.

"Stop her, Francis," shouted the clockmaker.

"Send the bots with her. She won't be stopped. I'll stay," Francis repeated.

"And so will I," said Rose as she also jumped down from the truck and ran toward Persephone.

"Oh dammit. Go. I'll get my birds and gnats to follow after you and help guide the way."

Another roar emanated from the canyon below.

"That's him, I'm convinced that's Gideon," said Francis. "Dammit, clockmaker, you promised to help. Get your bots before it's too late for any of us."

Manfred pulled open one metal storage locker, removing four glass tubes. One by one, he unscrewed the lids and, commanded the little flying devices to *follow the angels and find Gideon.*

He sat on the tailgate of the van and watched as the ragtag band took off down the hill. Tabby appeared, and sat in his lap.

PERSEPHONE REACHED THE darkened courtyard past the lab and stopped to listen for another outburst to give her direction. Hearing his scream had been what she'd been hoping for—the sound of his voice again—but she had not expected, nor did she want to hear it here, as he was a prisoner.

At least he's alive!

The buzzing hoard of bots zoomed past her, turned left and headed directly toward a row of one-story buildings that looked like animal pens. She began to hear laughing and clanging of metal as a lighted torch illuminated a row of metal cells lined with dirty rags and straw. At the far end, a group of guards had unlocked one cage door and had descended on whomever was occupying that space.

The bots disappeared into the cell as well and soon guards began to run, several of them holding onto their eyes, or swatting swarming bugs under their clothing.

A body lay, bloody and motionless, on its side.

She was on him, lifting his head, which was hardly recognizable, his face and eyes had been so beaten. "Gideon, Gideon, my love."

She feared he was dead and her heart was in shreds. His lifeless head hung in her arms. She brushed his hair back from his forehead, and kissed him.

"It's me, Gideon. I am here," she said through tears as she rocked him. "I have come to take you home. To your *real* home." She kissed his ears, kissed both his swollen eyes and then his lips.

Francis and Rose appeared at the cell.

"Francis! I think he's gone!" she sobbed. "Oh my God, I'm too late. Gideon's dead. We're too late."

Francis attempted to pick him up by the shoulders but Gideon's massive frame and dead weight proved too much. Even when Persephone tried to help him it was no use.

She hugged him, held his head between her palms and noticed some of her dust had escaped. Furious with herself for not having thought about it sooner, she rubbed her two fingers against her thumb and produced a palmful of golden dust, which she spread over his eyes, over his bloody shoulders and neck. She rubbed some of the glistening dust into his mouth and kissed him again. "Breathe, Gideon. Come back to me."

"Persephone, I think the best we can do now is just bring him home. He's gone, sweetheart."

"No! I will not give up. You go if you want, I'm staying with Gideon. I have no life without him."

She placed her palms on his shoulders. Francis held his head from rolling to the side, intending to help her bring his body to the truck. A light began to appear beneath and her healing powers glowed.

She heard a groan, and then Gideon opened his eyes and looked back to her face.

"Am I dead?" he whispered to her.

"No. No my love, you are alive, we both are alive." She was so happy she could hardly breathe.

"I'm dreaming this."

"No, Gideon. See? Francis is here, I'm here. We've got a truck to take you back home. But you're going to have to help us."

She heard the sounds of footsteps and knew they had run out of time.

"We won't make it unless you help, Gideon."

Francis added, "Hell, I always knew I was stronger than you. You big fat behemoth. Get off your butt and prove you're not dead, or we'll leave you here. I'll be the one to rescue Persephone while you rot in Hell."

That got Gideon to his feet. He growled and grabbed Francis by his bloody shirt. "You don't lay a finger on her, understand?"

The bots delayed a detail of six dark creatures who were armed with spears and swords. The little beasts stung their flesh, seeped acid into sensitive places like lips and eyes, and drilled tiny holes in their ears.

Gideon, with the aid of Francis under one shoulder, started limping into the night, following the two ladies. When he started to run, Persephone breathed a sigh of relief. Just before they reached the still waiting truck, Gideon had the strength to pick her up in his arms, and with one huge leap flew into the back of the truck and rolled with her in his arms. Francis was less graceful, and helped Rose up and then got an assist from Gideon.

The vehicle took off, lumbering down the bumpy dirt road, Persephone tucked safe in Gideon's massive arms.

"God, you smell good."

"And you don't," she said back to him.

CHAPTER 23

Three Months Later…

THE VINEYARD HAD started greening out again, Gideon's favorite time of year was spring. He finally had the time to tend his vines. Persephone was quick to learn everything about running a household, as well as a working vineyard, including working with a robotic crew of field hands Manfred had created for them.

With Manfred's usual sense of the bizarre, some of the warriors were outfitted with remnants of red leather bat wings that could serve as additional hands. Skin shades varied from blue to purple and bright pink. A cluster of birds hauled small implements and buckets of grain to the live chickens they raised. Tabby spent most of her days chasing baby chicks with real feathers, and a scent that drove her crazy. And though she was admonished several times, occasionally caught one.

The gnat bots were useful keeping pests from the

new leaves and Gideon knew they'd be invaluable chasing birds from the young fruit when the summer lengthened.

Francis's allergies completely cleared up once his right wing was also surgically removed and there didn't appear to be any lasting effects. Rose's grief over Dimitri's double-cross faded as she began to fall for the struggling Guardian.

One afternoon Persephone and Gideon were sitting on the back porch, drinking lemonade and watching the valley floor fall below them.

"Do you miss the Guardianship?" Gideon asked her.

"Not at all."

"You never talk about it."

"Everything that's important to me is in the future, Gideon. The Guardianship is in the past. I don't belong there any longer."

"Do you think He will allow that?"

"After all these months, with no contact, I think he's already telling us, we're on our own."

Gideon smiled smugly.

"You're up to something, Gideon. I can tell."

"Manfred would like to move his warehouse here."

"No. I will not live with that angel."

"Not *with* us, but on the property."

"Then he can have the little valley over that clump of trees so I don't have to look at him or his work. And I don't want to run an Emergency Room for freaks of the Underworld, Gideon. I didn't sign up for that."

"If he promises no interference?"

"We'll negotiate, then."

"You're a healer by trade, my angel. You make everything better. You could be Guardian to all the homeless beings who do not have someone to save them."

"No, I'm going to concentrate on you, Gideon. You are handful enough. And besides, your little bots are going to drive me crazy in a few months."

Gideon stood up. Persephone was smiling, but into her lemonade.

"Tell me that one more time."

"Manfred isn't the only one who can create creatures. But mine will be soft and pink. They won't ooze acid, but they'll smell bad sometimes. They'll drool. And they'll have the most wonderful father in the Universe."

"Seriously?"

"Seriously." She threw herself into his arms.

"Wonder what he'll be?" Gideon asked to the top of her head.

Persephone sighed. "Gideon, for all we've been

through and what we know of the Universe, does it really matter? *She'll* be ours to raise in the world of our own choosing."

True Love never dies.

ABOUT THE AUTHOR

S. HAMIL, Sharon Hamilton's twisted sister, writes paranormal romance with a central theme of the healing power of true love. Her characters from multiple worlds including Heaven and the Underworld are angels, dark angels, vampires and some who are not quite sure what they are. They follow a bumpy path to redemption, but not exactly what they taught you in Sunday School!

She loves hearing from her fans:
Sharonhamilton2001@gmail.com

Her website is:
sharonhamiltonauthor.com

Find out more about S. Hamil, her upcoming releases, appearances and news when you sign up for S. Hamil's newsletter.

Facebook:
facebook.com/SharonHamiltonAuthor

Twitter:

twitter.com/sharonlhamilton

Pinterest:

pinterest.com/AuthorSharonH

Amazon:

amazon.com/Sharon-Hamilton/e/B004FQQMAC

BookBub:

bookbub.com/authors/sharon-hamilton

Youtube:

youtube.com/channel/UCDInkxXFpXp_4Vnq08ZxMBQ

Soundcloud:

soundcloud.com/sharon-hamilton-1

S. Hamil's Rockin' Romance Readers:

facebook.com/groups/sealteamromance

S. Hamil's Goodreads Group:

goodreads.com/group/show/199125-sharon-hamilton-readers-group

Visit S. Hamil's Online Store:

sharon-hamilton-author.myshopify.com

Join S. Hamil's Review Teams:

eBook Reviews:
sharonhamiltonassistant@gmail.com

Audio Reviews:
sharonhamiltonassistant@gmail.com

Life *is one fool thing after another.*
Love *is two fool things after each other.*

REVIEWS

PRAISE FOR THE
GOLDEN VAMPIRES OF TUSCANY SERIES

"Well to say the least I was thoroughly surprise. I have read many Vampire books, from Ann Rice to Kym Grosso and few other Authors, so yes I do like Vampires, not the super scary ones from the old days, but the new ones are far more interesting far more human than one can remember. I found Honeymoon Bite a totally engrossing book, I was not able to put it down, page after page I found delight, love, understanding, well that is until the bad bad Vamp started being really bad. But seeing someone love another person so much that they would do anything to protect them, well that had me going, then well there was more and for a while I thought it was the end of a beautiful love story that spanned not only time but, spanned Italy and California. Won't divulge how it ended, but I did shed a few tears after screaming but Sharon Hamilton did not let me down, she took me on amazing trip that I loved, look forward to reading another Vampire book of hers."

"An excellent paranormal romance that was exciting, romantic, entertaining and very satisfying to read. It had me anticipating what would happen next many times over, so much so I could not put it down and even finished it up in a day. The vampires in this book were different from your average vampire, but I enjoy different variations and changes to the same old stuff. It made for a more unpredictable read and more adventurous to explore! Vampire lovers, any paranormal readers and even those who love the romance genre will enjoy Honeymoon Bite."

"This is the first non-Seal book of this author's I have read and I loved it. There is a cast-like hierarchy in this vampire community with humans at the very bottom and Golden vampires at the top. Lionel is a dark vampire who are servants of the Goldens. Phoebe is a Golden who has not decided if she will remain human or accept the turning to become a vampire. Either way she and Lionel can never be together since it is forbidden.

I enjoyed this story and I am looking forward to the next installment."

"A hauntingly romantic read. Old love lost and new love found. Family, heart, intrigue and vampires. Grabbed my attention and couldn't put down. Would definitely recommend."

PRAISE FOR THE
SEAL BROTHERHOOD SERIES

"Fans of Navy SEAL romance, I found a new author to feed your addiction. Finely written and loaded delicious with moments, Sharon Hamilton's storytelling satisfies like a thick bar of chocolate." —Marliss Melton, bestselling author of the *Team Twelve* Navy SEALs series

"Sharon Hamilton does an EXCELLENT job of fitting all the characters into a brotherhood of SEALS that may not be real but sure makes you feel that you have entered the circle and security of their world. The stories intertwine with each book before…and each book after and THAT is what makes Sharon Hamilton's SEAL Brotherhood Series so very interesting. You won't want to put down ANY of her books and they will keep you reading into the night when you should be sleeping. Start with this book…and you will not want to stop until you've read the whole series and then…you will be waiting for Sharon to write the next one." (5 Star Review)

"Kyle and Christy explode all over the pages in this first book, *[Accidental SEAL]*, in a whole new series of SEALs. If the twist and turns don't get your heart jumping, then maybe the suspense will. This is a must read for those that are looking for love and adventure with a little sloppy love thrown in for good measure." (5 Star Review)

PRAISE FOR THE
BAD BOYS OF SEAL TEAM 3 SERIES

"I love reading this series! Once you start these books, you can hardly put them down. The mix of romance and suspense keeps you turning the pages one right after another! Can't wait until the next book!" (5 Star Review)

"I love all of Sharon's Seal books, but [SEAL's Code] may just be her best to date. Danny and Luci's journey is filled with a wonderful insight into the Native American life. It is a love story that will fill you with warmth and contentment. You will enjoy Danny's journey to become a SEAL and his reasons for it. Good job Sharon!" (5 Star Review)

PRAISE FOR THE
BAND OF BACHELORS SERIES

"[Lucas] was the first book in the Band of Bachelors series and it was a phenomenal start. I loved how we got to see the other SEALs we all love and we got a look at Lucas and Marcy. They had an instant attraction, and their love was very intense. This book had it all, suspense, steamy romance, humor, everything you want in a riveting, outstanding read. I can't wait to read the next book in this series." (5 Star Review)

PRAISE FOR THE
TRUE BLUE SEALS SERIES

"Keep the tissues box nearby as you read *True Blue SEALs: Zak* by Sharon Hamilton. I imagine more than I wish to that the circumstances surrounding Zak and Amy are all too real for returning military personnel and their families. Ms. Hamilton has put us right in the middle of struggles and successes that these two high school sweethearts endure. I have read several of Sharon Hamilton's military romances but will say this is the most emotionally intense of the ones that I have read. This is a well-written, realistic story with authentic characters that will have you rooting for them and proud of those who serve to keep us safe. This is an author who writes amazing stories that you love and cry with the characters. Fans of Jessica Scott and Marliss Melton will want to add Sharon Hamilton to their list of realistic military romance writers." (5 Star Review)